THE
RETURN

by

JOSEPHINE SELLERS

Illustrations by Lisa Dickinson

Published by
Wessex Aquarian, P.O. Box 1059,
Sturminster Newton, Dorset,
DT10 1YA

Published in the UK 1990

Copyright Josephine Sellers 1990

Edited by John E. J. Lloyd

Printed in Great Britain by Butler & Tanner Ltd, Frome and London

THE RETURN

DEDICATION

**I dedicate THE RETURN to Brian, my loyal,
loving and hardworking husband.**

The Well

**Thanks to
Evelyn Payne, Cyril Jarman, Bob Sephton, John Lloyd
and Harry Johnson for all their practical help and
encouragement
and for their written contributions to
THE RETURN**

Foreword

by Harry Johnson

*Harry has over twenty years experience in the fields of philosophy,
metaphysics and parapsychology. He developed his own psychic abilities in England, and later became a qualified medium at the Arthur
Ford Foundation in the USA. As a teacher of the Silva Method of
Mind Control, and a Fellow of the College of Psychic Studies he has
lectured widely, both here and abroad. As the reader will discover, he
has no small part to play in my story.*

The greatest problem to be overcome by the potential medium
is the fear of 'possession'. The very idea of allowing your body to
be invaded and used by someone other than your self is, to say the
least, unwelcome to most of us. You wonder if the stranger might
misuse your body in some way or leave behind some harmful
residue effect. In addition, what would happen if the new incum-
bent refused to vacate your body at the end of the tenancy? You,
being out of it, might never again be able to get back in.

These fears stem from the commonly held view that your body
is the temporary vehicle of your soul, spirit, mind, higher self –
call it what you will – the essential and immortal YOU.

The common tendency is to look upon the body as if it were a
car, as if it were created by an agency other than oneself. You
merely possess a car, and then use it. If you lend it to someone else
they might damage it or even steal it. You might be prepared to
lend it to a friend in an emergency, but to trust your body with a
stranger, that is surely too much of a risk?

Yet there are many people who have been acting as mediums for
decades. They show no ill effects. On the contrary, they are often
looked on as sources of help when their friends experience
adversity.

Mediumship is the ability to receive information from other
minds, and it is natural to everyone in some degree. Those born

vii

with a high degree of ability are able to produce results despite the fears engendered by the 'temporary vehicle' idea. Josephine Sellers is to be congratulated for maintaining a belief in her intuitive abilities whilst playing a full part in the society that treats such talents disparagingly. What I had to offer her was a new pattern of thinking; a philosophy that, once accepted, eliminated the fears inherent in the 'temporary vehicle' way of looking at life.

That pattern of thinking is summarised below. As an unusual philosophy it will raise many queries among those of analytical bent. To potential mediums though, it provides ideas which can be seized upon, and then expanded and used by their own minds to bring about the development they desire.

'Your body is the result of your mind continually patterning matter in order to represent and maintain one aspect of itself in *this* reality. This creation by your mind is unique and cannot be duplicated or appropriated by any other mind.

Your mind, often called the soul, is able to obtain information from other minds, some of which may once have patterned bodies that are now dead. Mediumship, in all its aspects is the result of telepathic abilities natural to *all* minds.'

Preface

This book is a true account of strange events that have taken place in my life and that of my immediate family. These events add strength to the theory that life is a continuing and developing cycle of energy-experience through time. Reincarnation, karma, ancient sites and communication with entities from another realm are all a part of my story. I have been able to prove some of the psychic information which I have received by searching through historic records.

The greater part of this story, and the events it covers, took place in a very old thatched cottage in a Dorset village. Our move to this very particular spot was fortold by a number of independent sources. The purpose behind our return, for so it turned out to be, became known to us but only after many difficulties. We were also told of impending battles with planners and developers, and the problems they would meet in their attempts to desecrate the ancient site.

The story also describes my friendship with a Dorset country parson some four hundred years ago. The reason for the rekindling of this friendship is to give evidence to as many people as I can reach with this story that there is far more depth to life than would appear on the surface. The Rev William Thomas has much to tell that could help us greatly in coping with the pressures and influences of life today.

I have met and made many good friends over the period of time these events have taken place. Without their support and encouragement, this book would not have been written. They have offered me practical assistance and most of all they have worked alongside me as I have tried to unravel the mystery that has unfolded. The experiences which I and my family have been through, as a result of the following events have sometimes been hard. But they, and my supporting friends have shared my burden during these difficult times. Deep discussions and examination of the facts as they were revealed, made it apparent to us all that the events that have taken place were more than strange coincidences, they hold a deep and universal significance for all of us.

This book records events which have taken place in my life since early childhood. The events had psychic connections which gradually, over a long period of time, began to interelate with each other to produce evidence of earth energies, previous existence, and communicated wisdom. I think even the most hardened cynic would find it difficult to scorn or reject the whole of my story, there would seem to be so much to lose, and so little to gain by doing so.

The final chapter includes written pieces by friends of mine who are all experts in their own particular fields of paranormal phenomena. The articles in this chapter will be of help to anyone who is unfamiliar with psychic mediumship, healing, dowsing, and other aspects of that emerging spiritual age of which we are part, the New Age or the Aquarian Age.

Introduction

Today is Friday 16th December 1988 and now I am ready to to tell my story. It was five years ago on Monday 15th Jan.1984 that I felt driven to take up pen and paper.

'I know I must start to write. The reason for so doing is not clear, but I know I must write a story about the value of psychic evidence'

I had the feeling around that time that something was about to happen in my life. I knew the past had a bearing upon what was going to happen in the future and I felt an overbearing need to recall events from childhood that would eventually relate to an end result which was as yet unknown. I knew then that I wanted the writing to be a piece of work that would help to enlighten and inspire its readers just as many books about the paranormal had done for me over the passed few years.

The last five years for me have been an amazing journey. I had at the outset, little doubt about the fact we all live many many times in different circumstances and different situations. However, my greatest frustration at that time was my inability to be able to convince anyone else. The events of the past five years have only served to confirm my understanding and they have given me, I think, sufficient reason to lay before others evidence which will help them to question for themselves where the true depth in life lies.

To give my reader an insight into the kind of person I am, and how I think and live, I had best first return to my childhood.

I had a normal and happy childhood. There were however two events that occurred in those early years which have always remained firmly in my memory. The first experience took place when I was about seven years old. One night I awoke from sleep to find the bedroom flooded in lilac and purple light. Alarmed and frightened, I screamed out to my parents as I felt sure the electrical sockets in the room must have been faulty. The intensity of the light seemed to me as if it were electrical and charged with brilliant power. My parents rushed up to my room when they heard my screams, and after calming me down they assured me that there was no electrical problem. In later years they explained to me that at that time I had been having childhood health problems with my ears, nose and throat and that they had asked for absent healing for me from a friend of theirs who was a powerful healer. Their explanation of my frightening experience was that I actually had been able to see the healing energies being directed towards me by the process of absent healing. I have since learned that young children are often visually quite psychic in early years until the more material influences of culture and upbringing repress their sensitivity.

The second event, which I later understood to have psychic implications under what is termed an 'out of body experience', happened when I was about eleven years old. I was staying with an aunt whilst my mother was in hospital having an operation. One morning, while we were out shopping together in the local town, I was suddenly aware that I was rising out of my body to about twenty feet above it. It was warm and bright and I could see myself and my aunt walking along the street side by side. I felt totally disconnected from the world beneath me. The sound of the traffic was deadened, and my aunt's voice seemed far, far away. I felt contented and peaceful. After a short while I felt myself dropping back into my body. I could not understand what had happened to me. Bewildered and frightened I pretended that I was feeling ill, and asked if we could go home. I am not sure why I did not tell her what had just happened to me but I think I felt that she would not believe me. The one outstanding memory of this experience was the brilliance and warmth of the environment I had felt whilst rising above my own physical body. This only happened once during childhood, although it has occurred several times in later life. Many years later my own daughter had a very similar experience when we were walking the dogs in a local park. Thankfully she told me as soon as she dropped back into her body, and I was able to explain to her that it was quite alright and that it happened to many people, including myself.

It was during this period of my childhood that I very often had the strange feeling of being watched by a clergyman. At the time I was attending Sunday school. I had no knowledge of psychic communication for it was a subject people just didn't talk about, so I had to try and work things out on my own. In trying to explain this sensation to myself I assumed, in my child's mind, that it was our local vicar who could somehow manage to monitor my daily pursuits whilst engaged in his everyday life. Unlikely as it may seem, it was the only explanation I could place upon my experiences and sensations.

Such feelings seemed to be an intrusion into the freedom of my childhood. The 'presence' ever watching over me seemed to encourage me to take care of my behaviour and to develop a powerful conscience. Not so much a guilty conscience, as an inner feeling of what seemed to be the right or the wrong thing to do at the time. Further on into this story, the presence of this clergyman unfolds into a strange psychic relationship.

The final deep rooted memory I have of the inner feelings of my childhood is of an incident at about the age of twelve. I seemed to become aware that I had to work hard at my education to achieve success as I felt that I had something important to do in my later life. It was difficult then, as it is now, to put these inner instincts or feelings into words, for I had no idea what is was that was so important for me to do. However I responded to my intuitions, and made a quite dramatic advance in my academic work, moving two 'streams' up the school ladder in a three month period, a progress that would normally have taken as much as two years. After that, life became a serious and worldly affair. I gained good results, and left school to become a legal secretary in the City of London, until marrying at an early age.

Looking back now it is clear to see that I was tuned into my inner self in those early years and was responding, if unconsciously, to deep intuitions. This would generally seem to have been the case throughout my life, to a greater or lesser extent. However, as my tale relates, I have learned to become much more aware of these intuitions.My reactions are much more conscious and I am actually able to put these inner promptings to good use. I know now, from the experiences of the past few years that we are all born with a powerful intuition which can be of enormous benefit throughout our worldly lives if only they can be recognised by our culture. If these talents can be accepted and encouraged in early childhood, if we as adults can refrain from forcing our own beliefs upon our children and allow them to develop their own sensitivity, much sadness can be avoided in later life.

Chapter 1

My husband Brian and I met as teenagers and married young on the 3rd September 1965. He was my one and only serious boyfriend. During the years of our developing relationship we rarely discussed anything to do with psychic matters, though he was aware of my parent's interest in the subject. He does not remember any particularly strange or psychic experiences from his childhood, but always had a deep inner conviction of right and wrong. As for myself, during my teenage years I was more concerned with enjoying life, and after the experiences of my early years, had not experienced anything out of the ordinary.

It was during the early days of our marriage that I began to experience memories of a previous existence. These memories were of a grand lifestyle in sharp contrast to the small house and few possessions of our first struggling years. I could recall myself as a young lady dressed in long elegant clothes with long and beautifully coiffured hair. I lived in a grand country house, and I remember waking up in a four poster bed, with breakfast brought to me on a silver tray. From the casement window I could see a beautiful garden in which I would sometimes ride in a horse drawn carriage. I could recollect instructing somebody to have my grey horse saddled ready for me to ride. In our somewhat austere early marriage surroundings, I used to tease Brian by saying I was used to a far grander lifestyle than he could provide me with.

It was not until after the birth of our first child, a girl, Lisa, that I suddenly became interested in exploring psychic phenomena. I felt very much that I would like to visit a psychic medium to see what I might learn. I asked Brian if he would come with me and he agreed, though he admitted that he did not think much of such people. With the help of my parents it was not difficult to track down and make an appointment with a very well known international medium, Mr B. His performance certainly lived up to his celebrated reputation. He startled us with the highly accurate and detailed psychic information that he received about both of us, past and present. This information was of a personal nature and nobody but Brian and I could have known about it. We were also given forecasts for our future together.

At the time of our visit Brian and I were living at Uxbridge, just outside London. Mr B. told us of a move in future years to a county with a coastal border. A good part of Brian's working life, he said, would be spent designing at a drawing board. Brian was told that he would become well known for the work he carried out and that one day we would own undulating land of a considerable acreage in this coastal county. This forecast for the future seemed most unlikely to us. Brian was at that time working in an office carrying out clerical work and the idea of doing work of a remotely artistic nature had not entered his mind, nor did he consider that he had any such abilities. We felt the information did not relate to Brian at all, but possibly to my own brother who was already working as a textile designer so it was put to the back of our minds and it was only many years later that we were to realise its startling accuracy.

Mr B. told us that we were soul mates and had deliberately chosen to return together to earth to share our lives for a particular reason. The reason was not given. Over the following years this was something many mediums told us, although none could or would tell us the purpose of this return. I suppose that was for us to discover, through inner search.

After this visit, I decided to tell Brian's mother where we both had been. I suppose I expected her to be rather shocked and was very taken aback when she replied that she and her sisters had been having psychic experiences for many years. It was a situation she had kept very much to herself, so much so that even her own son was not aware of it. She has a tendency to foresee future events, an ability which even today she finds disturbing. She will see or sense a disaster and the form it will take, but has little idea of when or where it will happen, or the people who will be involved. Brian never had thought very much of psychic mediums. Their failures always seemed more obvious than their successes, but much of his scepticism vanished after our visit to Mr B., and his interest was greatly aroused. From that day on we began to take a far greater interest in the subject and I in particular began to read the first of a long chain of books about it. Through this interest we have met many people who have been strongly gifted with psychic powers, and I became particularly interested in the gift of healing (see Chap 17).

Throughout my childhood I had received healing, either by contact healing, in which the healer actually lays hands on the patient, or by absent healing when the healing process is projected, as it were, over long distances to the subject. I always found that contact healing given to me in childhood made me feel very warm and happy and sleepy. One very rewarding experience occurred when I asked for absent healing from an internationally known psychic healer for a very dear, lifelong friend of mine who had suffered a severe mental breakdown. Within a few days the results were dramatic and she was released from a mental hospital having only seven days prior been committed for a three month stay. She told me some time later that she had sat on her bed one evening in that hospital, looked at all the sick minded patients around her and knew immediately she did not belong with them. From that time onwards her mental state became totally stable and has remained so ever since. I have to believe that the directing of healing energies towards her had achieved the desired results, as she had been disturbed for a considerable time. The confidence I gained from this experience lead me to seek absent and sometimes contact healing for a number of friends over the following years with very happy results.

In 1968, two years after the birth of our daughter, our second child was born, this time a boy, Paul. Eight months before he was born I had been told by another medium that my baby was going to be a boy and I was given the exact day and hour of his birth.

It seems that birth is no accident. It seems that a soul which is returning to an existence on Earth selects the circumstances of birth so that it may experience areas of human experience which have not yet been undertaken. This idea of the development of the soul is very ancient indeed and lies behind many of the Eastern religions. However I support it not because so many other people do so, but because it agrees with the experiences and intuitions that I have amassed over the years.

As a philosophy, or an understanding, it certainly does help people to come to terms with the tragedies of this life. If we accept, for instance, that people born into terribly crippled bodies or minds may have actually selected their lives for themselves, we would find it very much easier not only to help them overcome their afflictions, but also to relate to them as personalities. Our approach would not be crippled by maudlin and confused sentiments of pity and reproach, nor would we need to blame our god every time something goes wrong!

There is much evidence to support the theory of reincarnation, and I have met too many people with their own stories and experiences of it to discard it lightly. I must admit that I found the idea difficult to accept at first, in spite of my own experiences, but when I examined the reasons behind my resistance I came to the conclusion that it was simply because my religion and culture had condemned the idea. It was contrary to church doctrine.

Planetary situations at the time of birth also play a major part in determining the life experience patterns to follow, and the day, date and time of birth are also a major factor taken into consideration by a returning soul. The evidence of our son's birth emphasised the feasibility of such ideas.

It was soon after our son's arrival that Brian began to feel very restless in his office environment. He gave his circumstances much thought and then one day announced that he was going to leave the indoor office life behind and become a landscape gardener. Our respective parents were surprised and concerned, but my own reactions were closer to astonishment and alarm. We had two young children and a mortgage to cope with, and this announcement posed a severe threat to our financial future. However, he obviously had not made his decision lightly, and though he had had absolutely no training whatsoever, his mind was made up. I knew he had a great dislike for working inside and I also knew he wanted to work for himself and feel free. Who was I to stop him?

Our first winter was a lean one. We could afford no luxuries; every penny spent was counted and grudged. We spent, for us, a small fortune on tools and advertisements. The initial orders were not promising and Brian, working outside for the first time in his life, suffered so badly from bronchitis that the doctor feared pleurisy was on the way. This would return each winter, he assured us, if Brian continued to work outside. Fortunately we decided to ignore his advice, but they were worrying times.

I think that in our inner hearts we truly felt that we were on the right track, and an obstacle was something that just had to be overcome. To others at the time, and maybe even to ourselves, we probably appeared to be just plain obstinate. We often made mistakes, and some of them were very painful, but the rewards were a growing strength and confidence.

It was at this time that both our sets of parents retired and decided to move to Poole, in Dorset. Not long after they had all settled into their new homes we joined them for a holiday. It took only two such holiday visits to Dorset for Brian and me to realise that Dorset was where we wanted to bring up our children. Once we had enjoyed the delights of the Purbeck Hills, and seen the beauty of the Dorset coastline, the London suburbs suddenly seemed very undesirable.

To uproot from London meant having to leave the newly developed business behind. But the pull of Dorset was irresistible and by this time we were becoming inured to hardship. Brian reckoned that if he could start up a business once, he could do it again. It was at this time that we recalled the forecast of Mr B. some four years before. Brian was working on landscape design, and here we were thinking of moving to a coastal county. In case there may be sceptics who think we moved because the medium said we would, I would urge them to think a little deeper. Would you uproot everything and move to another part of the country, simply because somebody had said you would?

We sold our London house, bought a new house on the outskirts of Poole and Brian set to work to rebuild his business. The first six months were financially tight. They were anxious months, and we were both a little frightened at the big step we had made.

Chapter 2

Living in Dorset to us was a great delight. Our children loved being so close to the sea and we all enjoyed excursions to explore the unspoilt and uncommercialised areas of coastline and country-side. It was such a contrast to our environment in London and such a welcome change.

For the first six months of our arrival we focussed all our energies on the redevelopment of Brian's business, and on getting our home together. After that we had time to pursue our psychic interest. It was not difficult for us to make contact with like minded people, and we were soon introduced to a local medium who had a very good reputation for her ability to communicate through trance mediumship. (see Chap 17).

We invited Mrs M. to spend an evening with us, and as we had never watched a medium working at a trance level before we were most interested in what went on. She was a very friendly and jolly lady and we had a long and fascinating discussion about the whole art of mediumship before she got down to work. After a few minutes of silence she slipped gently into a trance state. As she began to speak, we noticed that her voice had dropped considerably in tone, and had assumed not only a masculine quality but a suggestion of a foreign accent. When we questioned her later, she explained that the guide who worked through her was an ancient Egyptian.

I should just explain here that all psychic mediums usually work through one or more particular guides and that in the case of trance mediumship the relaxed state of the medium enables the guide to speak direct, using the voice box of the medium, whereas in other forms of mediumship the medium will receive communication from the guide at a mental or inner level, interpreting and passing it on while in a conscious state.

Brian and I were quite astonished at the accuracy of the past and

6

present information coming to us through Mrs M. We had at the beginning of the evening, only discussed generalities for our policy when working with mediums has always been to give away as little as possible about ourselves. We can then assess the value of the information received. Some of the material given to us by this guide was personal and fairly trite, however what was convincing was that she was able to tell us 'how we ticked'. In other words the information was more spiritually based and concerned with our perception of life from an inward point of view.

During the course of the session she began to describe in great detail an old thatched cottage in Dorset, to which she said we would one day move. It is difficult to remember the details given today, however the one description that always has remained in our minds was that she told us we would be able to sit upon a little window seat built into the wall of the cottage and look across a rose bed just outside the window to see a bird bath set in a lawn. She said that when we could see this we would know we were in the right cottage. We were not entirely convinced as we had only been in our new home for such a short while and were very happy there. So we assumed that this was something that would maybe take place much later in our lives. It had been a very interesting evening and we had been impressed with the quality achieved through trance mediumship. We would now have to sit back and let the years pass to see if we would ever find that thatched cottage.

Brian continued to work hard at his business whilst I cared for the children now aged six and four. Every moment of our spare time however was spent outside, exploring and enjoying Dorset.

In 1973, as our son began to approach school age, I knew that for the first time in seven years I would have time to myself. I had no wish to return to secretarial work again and as I very much wanted to work and yet still remain at home when the children were around, I began to think out the best way of having my cake and eating it.

Although I can far more easily accept an inspired thought today and act upon it, a few years ago I had no such confidence. But one day I awoke and knew that I wanted to work with dried flowers and more particularly I wanted to produce collages with them. I had no idea how to get started. All I seemed to have within me was a love of flowers and colour which I assume came from my mother and grandparents who were all florists. This was not quite the same as working with dried flowers, and I had no idea whether I had any artistic leanings.

Before I could start to produce collages, I had to locate some dried flowers. This was not so easy fifteen years ago, for they were not as popular then as they are now. However Brian made some enquiries through his trade and I ended up with an introduction to a lady who had spent many years growing and preserving garden flowers in Dorset. She had now decided to retire, and was in the process of winding up her business. I wrote a letter to her and in return was invited to go and see her.

On that first meeting with her I felt totally lost and inadequate when confronted with her knowledge and skill. The flowers she had grown and preserved were magnificient. I could not believe such beautiful specimens existed. But I felt myself charged with enthusiasm at what I could see and I must say that her example has always been a driving force and inspiration behind my floral work as it has developed over the years. The generous way in which she passed on her knowledge to me, and the close interest she has always taken in my progress have helped to cement a friendship I shall always value.

Brian had given me £50. If he had given me £500 it would not have been enough, I wanted to buy everything in sight. But eventually I arrived home with my raw materials, bought some hessian, board and glue, stripped out the spare bedroom, set up a work bench and I was ready to start.

My progress was so slow, it took me weeks to develop a feel and an eye for what I knew I wanted to create. But gradually it started to happen and apart from the enormous worldly satisfaction I gained from producing something that pleased my eye, the inner satisfaction and pleasure was beyond description. I seemed to have opened my mind to a different dimension of thought and I felt as if I was coming alive. I can see now that I was begining to open up the creative side of my personality, which we all have but sadly too often neglect.

Soon I had produced some satisfactory results and was convinced I wanted to continue the collage work. It became obvious that if I was to master the art completely I would have to grow the flowers and preserve the flowers myself. So I paid another visit to my flower lady who was able to advise me as to the best varieties to grow and, most important of all, was able to pass on to me many of her secrets regarding the art of perfect preservation.

The months passed by, and as I was developing my floral abilities, other areas of our life were also beginning to show signs of movement. Brian and I had been exploring Dorset pretty thoroughly, and we were beginning to feel that we would prefer to live in a more rural and isolated environment. Life on a new housing estate had certain disadvantages for the children. In such close communities young children want to be out and playing with each other seven days of the week and it is difficult to maintain a degree of supervision and home discipline when they are living in a lively 'gang' society which sometimes lays too much stress on imitation. Consequently, we felt a more self sufficient family environment would be better for them. We were also ourselves starting to find estate life claustrophobic, especially after returning from our rural explorations.

We began to look for a new home in the country areas a few miles inland from Poole. One evening in the local paper, after several weeks of searching without success, we saw a thatched cottage advertised just a few miles away near Wimborne. We were very tempted to go and view it, but decided against it as we were a little worried about the expense involved in the upkeep of a thatched roof and it was also not in an area that particularly appealed to us. The paper got thrown away and the idea put out of our minds. However, several days later whilst I was preparing the evening meal, I got the most overpowering urge to retrieve the newspaper from the dustbin. Rummaging around in all the rubbish, I eventually found it, and there and then rang the estate agent for an appointment to view the cottage. Something had prodded and pushed me, I had responded, and two days later Brian and I were on our way to view the cottage.

Chapter 3

We approached up a long and winding tree lined driveway which opened into a horseshoe shaped garden with a thatched and white-washed cottage standing right in the middle. It was so quaint, just like having stepped back into the past. We were greeted at the very low front door by a friendly, elderly lady who invited us inside. What a warmth of atmosphere we encountered as we stepped inside! Brian and I both had the strangest feeling flood through us. It felt as if we had come home. We had returned! This is the only possible way to describe the strange sensation we both felt as we walked through that low front door into the hallway of that ancient cottage. Our hostess led us through into her dining room and there was the little window seat built into the wall of the cottage. Through the window we could see across the rose bed to the bird bath set in the front lawn. The exact description we had been given by that ancient Egyptian guide speaking through his channel.

From the dining room we were shown around the rest of the cottage with its low beamed ceilings, and sloping bedroom floors. It was a classical English cottage, and Brian and I had fallen in love with it. To the front was a pretty garden with an enormous and ancient pear tree in the middle whilst the remainder of the garden was set out to rows of vegetables and fruit cages. A natural hedge enclosed the garden and beyond it as far as we could see were farm fields. It was a truly idyllic environment, just what we had been looking for. The owner took us back inside, sat us by the open fire and made us a cup of tea. We told her we wanted to buy the cottage but explained that we had first to sell our house which we would put on the market immediately. We agreed to pay the price she was asking and our offer was accepted and as she was in no great rush to sell,she was prepared to wait until we could find a buyer for our house. It was clear to see that she was very fond of the cottage herself and was only leaving because it was becoming to big a task for her to manage alone. It was important to her that the new owners should appreciate the cottage and would want to go on caring for it as she had done.

It was time to get out of the armchairs and leave and although we felt slightly uncomfortable to be sitting in this lady's home, who we had only just met, it was the most difficult task to lift ourselves out of those chairs and go. We both felt we wanted to stay, and as we eventually drove away down the long and winding driveway, we were very determined to take ownership of that cottage as soon as possible.

It was August 1973 when we found the cottage and it took us until February of the following year to find a buyer for our house. Those six months seemed endless, so much did we want to get to that cottage.However, eventually we were on our way. At the beginning of May we changed homes, just in time to plant out that first crop of flowers that I had grown in seed trays in the garden of our home in Poole. The cottage had one acre of garden and I was in a hurry to put it to good use.

Our feelings upon arriving to live at the cottage can never be forgotten. The sun shone brightly upon that May day. The garden was in a very natural state. Bluebells and daffodils grew at random from the banks and lawns. Azaleas and rhododendrons were in full bloom, the fruit trees were covered in blossom. It seemed like paradise to us and such a welcome change after living in a noisy modern housing estate.

Just one week after moving in, we invited the medium who had described the cottage in such detail some two years prior, to visit us and celebrate with a bottle of champagne. We all toasted the cottage, standing beneath the magnificient limbs of the huge pear tree set in the front lawn. She asked if she could attempt further trance communciation work for us and we agreed. Her guide said that we would be carrying out major structural alterations to the cottage over the coming years and we were told that because of what we would achieve whilst living there, we would become famous and as a result would travel around the world to meet other people in some similar connection. What exactly we were going to achieve was not indicated. We were also told that as the years passed by we would gradually take control of the fields around the cottage because of a connection we would have with horses.

Those early days in the cottage were so enjoyable, full of fun and hope. Yet all the time the future was slightly tinged with financial anxiety. We had taken on a considerable commitment with the

11

move and our security was very much dependent upon Brian's fluctuating work load. There were times when I felt very insecure and as I knew I could not bear to have to leave the cottage and its surroundings, I suppose the insecurity was also tinged with fear. But we had to maintain faith in our intuition, and our long term future. Success had been predicted. This cottage had been described to us in great detail prior to our finding it and here we were now living in it. These facts served to pull Brian and I through some very difficult business and financial times over the following years and helped to give us the courage to persevere when the odds were stacked heavily against us.

The children at first missed their friends and found it difficult to depend upon themselves and each other for companionship and play. However, they adapted in time, and now, when they look back on their dayspring days, they can see how their life at the cottage had such a strong influence upon the type of people they have grown into. Their thoughts, their view of the world and the people in it, their perceptions of the past and the future are all strongly flavoured by the peace and atmosphere of our cottage near Wimborne.

Not long after our arrival at the cottage, we began to feel the need to acquire more animals. We had arrived on that first day with just one cat. First of all came a beautiful Old English Sheepdog, called Samuel, then another one called Benjamin arrived to keep him company. We were given another cat and collected several rabbits and guinea pigs.

There can be no doubt that the presence of all those animals gave to us a quality of life that is surely missing when animals are absent. Because of the experience of living with them all I could not imagine any part of the rest of my life being complete without sharing my home with them. They have so much to offer that brings quality to human life and are a magnificent way of teaching children a gentleness and sense of responsibility. Eventually we also ended up with three beautiful horses, who arrived at two yearly intervals and then, to complete the forecast of so long ago, we took over the grazing tenancies on the adjoining land.

Our Animals

Chapter 4

We had not been living at the cottage for very long before Brian and I began to experience a rather strange phenomenon. It was something that remained with us all the years we were there and as our son grew older, it started to affect him also. We found that when we travelled a few miles away from the cottage, after a short while we would experience a pulling sensation in the solar plexus area, it was also accompanied by an overwhelming desire to return home. I would find myself driving home at a ridiculous pace and I would have to force myself to reduce speed. However, we did find that if we travelled a considerable distance away, say over twenty five miles or so, the sensation disappeared and would re-occur again when back inside the twenty five mile radius. Later in these pages I will explore these sensations, for they were no coincidence.

During the first five or six years of living in the cottage, we came into contact with many mediums and other people who were psychically orientated in other directions. The reader may be surprised to know that nowadays there are great numbers of people in our society who experience psychic phenomena, and there is no longer any reason for anyone who has these talents or skills to feel alone and solitary.

All the mediums we had contact with, whether they came to the cottage or whether we met them elsewhere, kept giving the same very similar information to us about something we were going to achieve whilst living there. Some felt we were going to take ownership of the surrounding fields and use them for a purpose. We were also told of large numbers of visitors coming to the cottage in the future and wheelchairs and disabled people were mentioned.

All I can say is that there was most certainly a degree of continuity in each piece of information we received. As the years and my story

The Shop in the Garden

progress, it is clear that our interpretations and those of some of the mediums were not always accurate. As a result we sometimes experienced considerable frustration, confusion and unhappiness. It was not until I learned to work at a far deeper psychic level myself that the way ahead became clearer.

I had continued to work at the development of my dried flower collages since our arrival at the cottage. Harvests of flowers from the garden were prolific and the output of collages soon made it necessary for me to find a sales outlet. In the early stages I took my wares to the local markets to sell to the tourists. But I soon tired of having to travel to different towns every day and thought how nice it would be if I could sell direct from the cottage. I applied to the Local Planning Authority to run a Cottage Industry with a small shop in the garden and was granted three years of temporary planning. We put up an attractive chalet in the garden and from this little shop I sold my dried flower collages and arrangements surrounded by the flower beds which contained the next year's raw materials.

It was as people began to come and look at my shop, that I

15

became aware that the environment of the cottage and its garden had an effect upon them. So many remarked that when they walked up our long and winding driveway they felt they were entering a different world. Many begged to be allowed to linger because of the peace they felt there, and many returned time and time again to enjoy the sensation. It was because of this that Brian and I began to feel that there was something unique about this small area of land upon which we lived. People in general were drawn towards it. Friends who came to stay said they went home feeling charged and refreshed, and on top of it all there was that strange magnetic pull we both felt when we were away from home.

Brian and I tried to put two and two together. We had been told we were to take control or possibly even ownership of the adjoining land. We were in fact already in control of it through our grazing tenancies and so we began to imagine what we would do with it if by some miracle we one day had enough money to buy it. The only way we felt capable of making use of the additional land would be to extend the very beautiful garden that Brian already had made. We even went as far as contacting the owner of the adjoining land, with a view to a possible purchase. Our requests were always rejected and we were told that he would only sell when he was good and ready, and even then at its highest possible price for housing development. Sadly, this was as we expected. The developers were already eating into Dorset and it was only a matter of time before their machines would be chewing away at our own ancient site.

For three years I ran my cottage industry on a temporary planning basis and then the time arrived when we either had to renew it or expand and apply for full planning. With faith in our future we applied to increase the scale of the venture considerably and once again our application was successful. We would now be allowed to build a far larger shop and I could invite other craftsmen to sell and work with me. However, at this stage we did not have enough money and for the time being I would have to continue to work alone and hope that one day I might be able to expand.

Meanwhile my psychic life was not being neglected. There are today many groups of people throughout the country who have got together to develop their psychic talents. Usually these development circles are run by an accomplished medium who teaches and advises the other members. The aim of these groups is not to produce more mediums, but to help those many, many people who have undoubted psychic talent and need to develop it for their own peace of mind, or even their own physical health. The end result, if all goes well, is a receptive person whose intuitive processes are

16

finely tuned and do not require the services of a medium to interpret them.

One of these development circles was quite nearby. I joined it, and learned a great deal that helped me to come to terms with my own psychic energy. We all began to improve over the course of several months, and information began coming through from members of the group that directly related to our adventure at the cottage. I must stress that none of the members had been to the cottage, or knew anything about it.

The information they kept receiving appeared to come from a little old man who said that he had once lived at the cottage. He kept trying to tell me that there was something of great value buried at the cottage. He also appeared visually to a psychic friend of ours who happened to be visiting us at the time, and he once again passed the same message.

Buried treasure! Brian and I were more than intrigued by this news, which surfaced again and again over the next few years, and which was going to cause us great confusion and frustration.

Our first reaction was to start digging.

'But where on earth do we start?' I asked Brian.

'Well, where do you think he'd have buried it, outside or inside?'

It had not even occured to me that it might be inside.

'There are no foundations, these stone slabs are just laid on the original earth floor, and this is the only ground floor room of the original cottage.'

'Yes, but we can't dig up our dining room, just like that!'

'Why not?' replied Brian, ' If we try outside it might be anywhere, if we try inside, this is the only place it could be. Anyway, if it rains we can go on digging.'

It occured to me that there were not many people who had the privilege of even being *able* to dig up their dining rooms.

So we dug it up.

First we removed the stone slabs that covered the old earthen floor. We then piled the furniture and the animals around the sides of the room and set to work, the children joining in with unusual enthusiasm for, as Brian remarked, it's not often you get the chance to pull down the family home. Most parents resent even a broken teacup!

By tea time we had a sizeable hole in the middle of the floor, and the furniture and the animals were beginning to disappear behind the mounds of earth. But we ploughed furiously onward, ever urged by the seductive bleepings of a metal detector we had borrowed. Alas for the Siren's song! All that came to the surface were huge chunks of ironstone, probably used as firmings for the ancient mud walls.

We had our tea sitting on top of the dining room table, which was perched precariously on the edge of the crater. While we ate, the dogs, cats and children happily puddled away in the gaping mess.

And then to our horror we saw that the hole was steadily filling up with water! Frantically we worked to fill it in, but it was with no great confidence that we eventually laid the flagstones back in their proper place. For some time we feared that the monster beneath the house had been liberated, but as the days passed there was no sign of nastiness creeping up between the stones and life resumed it's normal tenure. At least the children and the animals had had a wonderful day, but the enigma was going to remain with us for quite some time before we eventually solved it.

Chapter 5

In the Autumn of 1982, a very good friend of mine gave me the name of a new medium now working in the Bournemouth area. This friend was himself a most capable medium and as he had seen this lady working in public and was impressed with her. I took her name and address and put it to one side, thinking I might well contact her one day when the time felt right. Some nine months later I telephoned and made an appointment to see her in Bournemouth.

It was a hot and sunny early summer's day. The door of the flat was opened by a bright and breezy lady who introduced herself as Eve and invited me inside. I was taken into a room, full of house plants and with rows and rows of books upon shelves. The windows were wide open and there was a continuous roar of heavy traffic from the main road below. Eve was very friendly and relaxed. I was invited to find a comfortable seat and instructed not to tell her anything about myself before she started to work psychically for me. At this stage, she did not even know my name. Eve offered to make a tape recording of our meeting as she felt sure I would never be able to remember everything that I might be told. I was impressed by her approach and felt confident that the meeting was going to be fruitful.

My experiences with mediums have always been positive and I suspect that this is because my own psychic energy reacts strongly with that of the medium and will invariably produce a result. But some people are disillusioned and this can be for a variety of reasons. For a start their own attitude may be negative, and this can affect the performance of a medium, for we are dealing now not with a comfortable scientific world of cause and effect, but one in which our deep feelings can quite unconsciously wield the energy of a powerful generator. Sometimes the medium is not particularly efficient or confident, and when things are not going right this can lead to dishonesty and deception. But most people who are looking for a service will first look for someone who has a good reputation. The same applies to mediums, and I would say to those who want to make contact with one, ask around first before making your appointment.

As I had anticipated, the quality of information given was excellent. I was immediately told of my connection and work with flowers. A detailed physical and personal description was given of my deceased grandfather with information about his business connections within the florist trade. I was told that my floral work was being influenced by a young Japanese lady, who had been around me for many years. This was remarkable news because as a child, a contact healer had once told me of a Japanese girl who was close to me. He also gave me a pastel sketch of this Japanese girl which my Mother has kept to this day. It did not surprise me at all to be told that there was an external influence behind my floral work. In fact I long ago come to a similar conclusion. This Japanese lady told me through Eve that to me my flowers were 'a way of religion'. If she meant this to mean that they brought me closer to my creator and my origins, then she was correct. I was told that the essence of my floral collages acted as healing therapy to those who bought them from me. I have since come to understand more fully what this means.

If thought contains energy in the same way that any other action does, then the care that goes into a creation is part of the energy of that creation. From the actual growing of a flower from seed, to the finished designed and arranged collage, the energy of care and thought has gone into every stage. My thoughts are contained within my finished creation, and the energy from them benefits those who are capable of absorbing the 'vibrations'. This principle of course applies to any creation. I think I begin to see now why people like to own old cars, and old wooden boats, and original paintings. Of course some capitalise on this desire and make money out of it but many, unconsciously perhaps, appreciate the latent thought-energy that has been poured into the creation. When everyone gathers together to bless a ship before sliding her into the water, does the outpouring of thought from that gathering form part of that ship, and all who sail in her?

But let us return to Eve. She then went on to describe a rather elegant young lady, living many years ago in a country house in Somerset. I was told this person was strongly connected to me. At the time, this information meant nothing to me. At the end of my meeting with Eve she told me that I was quite spiritually advanced and that I had been meant to make this contact with her to form 'a link in a chain of events'. On this point she either could not or would not elaborate other than to say that it was most necessary for us to have met.

We had got on very well together at that first meeting. I had to admit that I felt drawn towards her and I felt also that she could help me a lot more in my search. But search for what? At that time I did not know, except that I seemed to be looking for some kind of truth. I felt deep inside me that there was something I had to find out.We said our goodbyes and expressed the hope that we would meet again.

One month later I telephoned Eve and asked if she would like to come and visit Brian and me at our home, an invitation which she eagerly accepted. This meeting at our cottage was to produce the first of many psychic communications that we received through Eve. It was an evening early in August of 1983 that she first visited us. Apart from giving her our address I had told her absolutely nothing about our home. Within a few minutes of arriving Eve settled down in our small living room and got to work.

It may be helpful to explain at this point that there are many ways in which mediums can 'channel' communication from a spiritual source. They can be totally conscious and aware throughout the process, they can be in a deep trance and totally unconscious of what is going on, or they can work somewhere between these two conditions, that is in a state of high receptivity and yet at the same time in complete control of the proceedings. The type of actual communication can also vary within these various states. It may come through as something the medium 'sees' or 'feels', or as a relayed message in the third person – ' She says that she etc etc ...', or the medium may act as a mouthpiece through which the 'entity' actually speaks, during which time the medium's voice or face may undergo considerable change. I am not a practising medium myself, neither do I consider myself as yet to be par-ticularly skilled in that direction, but when I do undertake chan-nelling work I find that the most powerful impression that I retain after a session is that of 'feeling' or emotion, and it is surprising how much that offers as a clue to the entity who has made contact with me.

I think that at this stage I should make it clear that when talking or writing about psychic matters it can be very difficult to find the right language. So many of the words have unpleasant connections with lurid ghost stories, or with dire warnings from well meaning

21

A Roman Soldier

'experts' who really have little idea what they are talking about. 'Occult', 'spirits', 'entity', are but a few from that list, and I can only beg the reader not to be triggered into a negative reaction when I use a word which may not have the right feeling. Charity is called for here, and an understanding that many such words are used to describe things about which we know very little indeed.

Eve usually works in a relaxed state of awareness and describes what she can see and hear. On this first occasion at the cottage she told us that we were living upon a very ancient site, far more ancient than the four hundred years that the cottage had been there. Gradually she began to pick up entities from the past who had been connected to the cottage. One of the first to make himself known was a man who said he was of a military background and that he had been the owner of the cottage some years before us. He had bought the cottage for his retirement and had had great hopes for it but had died very shortly after arriving. He then went on to say that he enjoyed watching us carry out improvements to the cottage and the garden and that he liked to observe our children growing up, as he'd had no children of his own. When Brian and I later

22

checked the deeds of the cottage we found that the first owner, after it had been released from being a tithe cottage in 1945, was a retired army Colonel.

Eve went on to say that apart from the site of the cottage being very ancient, it was also a power site (see Chap 17) and for that same reason it had been lived upon and used for psychic orientation in previous times. She told us that she understood that Brian and I were the correct people to be in residence now. We then started to move further back in time. A Roman soldier showed himself to Eve, dressed in full uniform, and we were told that we were living upon some kind of Roman site, not a residential site but a Roman barracks. The soldier did not live here as such, but was on duty guarding the boundary line of a fortress or garrison. We were then told that we were living on or very close to a Roman travelling route, and that in the ground beneath us there could be found evidence of this Roman occupation.

As can be imagined, Brian and I were very excited by the quality of communication we were receiving. It was all so interesting and it was taking us into an area of exploration we could never have anticipated. Since we had arrived at the cottage we had been most curious to find out about its history. We knew it was about four hundred years old and that it had been an estate tithe cottage for most of that time, but we had not given any thought to a time before its existence. Eve herself was also fascinated by the information she was receiving and asked if we would consider allowing her to return again to work at a trance level of mediumship (see Chap 17). Under such conditions, she felt that it would be possible to improve the quality of communication considerably and we would be able to gain a deeper insight into the situation. She asked that she might bring along with her next time a friend who worked as a healer. She had only recently acquired the skill of working at trance level and she felt it advisable to have someone with knowledge and expertise to watch over her whilst she was in trance. We agreed to meet again in two weeks time and parted company greatly encouraged by our experience.

The day after Eve's visit, Brian and I set out to find as much as we could about the history of the area around our cottage. We ended up at Poole Museum were we found out that about half a mile from the cottage there had been a Roman fortress and that excavations had already been carried out there during the building of a bypass. We were already aware that a bridle track a quarter of a mile away from the cottage, along which we used to walk our dogs, followed the course of an old Roman road.

Many readers will, I expect, feel that Eve may have known about the Roman connection with the area before coming to see us. All I can say here is that this was not so and there was, and is, no question of deception. We were not paying Eve for all this work, and for her to spend her time and money in research, just to impress us, would have been a great waste of effort. I appreciate though that the problem of proving no deception is extremely difficult. When any hard facts are given during a communication they can only be proved by going to some form of existing record. As soon as that record is found, it can then be claimed that the medium knew all about it in the first place! Our case is no exception to this problem. On the other hand, the accuracies of the forecasts and prophecies that we received are much more difficult to discount, particularly as many of them were taped at the time and deposited with a local bank.

In 1988, a Roman military road was uncovered in the field behind our cottage, just fifty yards from our front door. Eve had told us we were living close to an ancient travelling route. It is unlikely that in August of 1983, she would have had access to that sort of information. She continued to give us more and more evidence which we were able to confirm through research. We were at the beginning of what was going to become a strange tale of reincarnation.

Chapter 6

It was an evening in late August of 1983 that Eve arrived to attempt trance communication. With her came her husband, Cyril the healer and his wife. We settled ourselves down in the lounge of our cottage with its heavily beamed ceiling and deep inglenook fireplace. After chatting a bit we all sat quietly in our armchairs as Eve started to relax sufficiently to move into a trance. We had placed a tape recorder close to her, as from now on we were going to record every meeting. After some ten to fifteen minutes of peaceful meditation, Eve began to speak very slowly in a noticably deeper and more masculine voice. This is what was recorded that evening:–

'There is such beauty here. An improvement from past years. The atmosphere is conducive to the work that will be done through-out the coming years. But I am forgetting that I must be a little more considerate to my hosts this evening.

I would greet the both of you and introduce myself. I am known to these that sit here with you as the Reverend Thomas. Our young control is becoming used to my touch and so I would be the first to entrance her, to give her the confidence and the state of peace within that is so necessary for the work that is being attempted. We are most aware of the pull to your heartstrings these last few years. Your patience has been tried as has also your devotion. We make no apologies for these matters for your own spirits (meaning our inner selves) are quite capable of understanding why this needs be so.

There was a time when the two of you were most familiar with these lands that are around you. There was a time when all but one of you that are gathered here, were quite familiar with each other, for you all belong to the same tribe of people. This may surprise you a little, but it should not, for have you not become aware that

The Old Inglenook

all things are planned for a greater reason than can be proved within one lifetime? I know that you have an appreciation of the arts of re-occuring lives and situations, but I would like you, though, to have an understanding why the fisher of men has drawn you together.

There was upon this ground a group of men of great wisdom. Some called them sages, it was a great time ago. I believe we could say within earth years that we are travelling back to a time that is well over three thousand years. In those times the area was sparsely populated. There were what one could term hermits around, and they would lead a singular life for a singular purpose. They were greatly skilled in the arts of obtaining and gathering information from the beginning of time and to take it way before into the time to come. It was their duty to place upon this land a covenant and this was done, and this land and its covenant must always, down through all times, be protected from those who are not of spiritual awakening.

We know that your knowledge goes reasonably deep and that your hearts and minds are pure. You have been well tested. For the responsibility that we would place upon your shoulders will be a heavy burden. There are the necessary tools locked within the bowels of the earth to provide in more than one direction, and we charge you with the future, for you will be granted some of those treasurers that are much admired upon your earth. These treasures are of little interest to we of spirit, though we have a deep respect for the problems of your material world. We know that dues must be met and we are thankful that you have given every last ounce of faith and coinage and trust into this project of the future. Your faith will be well rewarded.

There will be in the next five years, openings that will return in many fold that which you have freely given. We ask you to hold fast to your faith and to your trust. Do not allow it to be shaken for there is no need. All will, in due course of time, become upon your earth of such an awakening knowledge as to give you much happiness and business. As time goes by, others who are also able to be of use in this enterprise of the future will be drawn to you. Your little shoppe is a sweet beginning, but it is as the bee to the honey. We will show you in three years from now, that which will take you into the dawning of the new age for both of you. Your little shoppe will grow into something that will surprise even you. I thank you kindly for bidding me welcome, but now I know that you will be most pleased to hear another speak with you. I will just stand aside a little, but I will not leave. Those of you that are capable of seeing will see me standing between the chairs of the one that is the husband and the one that we use. For she is my charge this night.'

There was no one capable of seeing him that night, and in fact I have not yet visually seen him, though I have received mental pictures of other entities. Many years ago, quite out of the blue, a friend of mine remarked that she could see a priest-like figure standing beside me. He was dressed in black, with a brimmed hat, and he had some white cloth around his throat. I assume that this was the Reverend Thomas.

It can be seen from his remark:– 'Our young control is becoming used to my touch' that Eve had already had communication from this gentlemam before meeting Brian and me. My reader will recall that when I first visited Eve in her flat in Bournemouth, she had said that I was meant to meet her to form a 'link in a chain' although she could elaborate no further at that time and she also had no idea at that meeting that I would request to see her again. The only reason she was here this evening was because I had felt inwardly drawn towards her and because I felt she could help me further in

27

my search for answers to questions deep within me. It was now quite apparent to me why my meeting with her had formed the 'link in a chain of events'.

The Reverend Thomas 'stepped to one side', and a few seconds later we received the voice of a very pompous sounding gentleman coming through the voice box of Eve.

'She is pretty that one. Yes. I approve, I approve. Upon this site they had so many hags at times. Ancient crones, that were not much to look at. I prefer one such as you my dear that is pleasing on the eye. The stench here at times – phew! – makes one want to cover ones nostrils. But I would come in upon my horse for I had a house but five miles hence. I would come into this abode, for there was one who had a great deal of wisdom and she would help us with love potions and she would give us many potions to help us when we suffered with some awful diseases such as – they are really beyond me. I prefer to allow the women to do the caring and nursing, for it is not the place of a gentleman to be seen in the bedchamber of the sick. This old woman was different, although the smells at times were a little hard to bear.

She had words of great wisdom that I used to enjoy listening to and though I know now that it was a sin, she would give me potions that would help with the servants that got with child too often. You know I am sure what I am saying to you, for it is not for a gentleman to talk too closely of such matters. There were problems though, but this old crone would help us in many ways and I would sit around her hearth, most interested in what she would say to me, for though she was thoroughly uneducated and coarse in many ways, her wisdom was wide and great. It had its fascinations and without her aid, life would have been a great deal more complicated for the gentlemen of the countryside.

So we have much to be thankful for and you pretty young maid, have also got the capabilities of seeing that which is of other worlds as did the old crone, though your knowledge is not as deep as hers. You should work at those parts of you and then you would see more my dear. You would see others who also lived about here in my time. In those days we had quite a power of control upon the hills and valleys for miles around this cottage. The hamlet was owned by us, by my generation and by others of my family for many generations before me. It passed out of my family's control in the sixteenth century and you will find within your legal documents a multitude of changes after that.

I have watched your searching and been interested, but your documents are far from complete, for in the sixteenth century many were destroyed for all times. You are the rightful tenants of this property, I would say that to you, and here you must stay. And we will together make attempts to put right the wrongs so that your stay may be of a long period and satisfactory to both yourselves, and to us, who still watch and guard the true meaning and content of these lands.

The blessings of the Lord God will walk with you and the many who guard and guide your fortunes and shelter you in the storms, but the worst of them is now over for both of you, for though at this moment it would seem that both of you are greatly ravished by the strength of the storms that have hurtled and blown and stamped around you, take faith in the knowledge that the winds have abated and the sun is beginning to shine through the branches with a greater strength.

We bid you farewell our little princess, for that, to us, is what you are. Farewell'.

This presumably landed gentleman refers to us being 'greatly ravished by the strength of the storms that have hurtled and blown and stamped around you' and the Reverend Thomas says:- 'We are thankful that you have given every last ounce of faith and coinage and trust into this project of the future.'

So we, Brian and I, were here for a purpose! It was something to do with the cottage and the land. It required us to remain here for a while. I can now explain to my reader the correctness of these statements. Brian and I were prior to this evening, as you are already aware, quite sure ourselves as to the therapeutic value of the land upon which we lived. We had seen the reaction it had upon visitors to my shop. I have also told you of our approaches to the adjoining land owner, approaches to the local authority and the gaining of planning for a larger floral and general craft venture. All these actions were not only time consuming but also quite expensive to follow through and we were begining to feel the financial pressure. Brian was also finding that his business was not as profitable as it had been. Financial times in the country as a whole were difficult around that period of high inflation and recession. Many businesses were going under and we were hanging on by our finger tips.

When Eve withdrew from the trance state she seemed quite tired. Before leaving she gave us the tape recording of the session, telling us to contact her if we wanted to go on with the work. Left to ourselves we pondered on the extraordinary events of the evening. We felt stunned. We had not given any thought to such a depth of purpose in this life time and certainly we had not even considered what we might have done in any previous lives. It is not every day that a person receives such information, and it was most difficult to grasp or even accept the weight of the responsibility placed upon our shoulders. Indeed we did not accept it, we wanted further proof.

We also wanted to share the information with somebody else, if only to find out whether they thought it could be a possibility and so, a few days later we asked some of our closest family to listen to the tape. Mothers, fathers and Brian's sisters all listened and all were wary and concerned. We should be very cautious, they said, in case it was some kind of hoax that spirit entities might be playing on us.

We had asked for advice, but we only listened to it with half an ear. In spite of our anxiety we were intrigued, even excited, and having come this far we did not feel like turning back. We felt that we should follow it through if only to prove whether we were involved in some fantasy, or a different dimension of reality. We already suspected that this was no hoax, for much that had been said had touched upon our inner feelings. Somehow we felt that in coming to the cottage we had, in some strange way, returned home.

The statements made by the Reverend Thomas and the landed gentleman served to offer us comfort. However, as time goes on and my story progresses, it is clear to see that Brian and I put too much emphasis upon the possible financial rewards of our land. We believed that the situation would be taken care of for us. How wrong we were! Our worldly situation was ours to handle to the best of our ability. But we were tackling it without respecting the spiritual guidance that was available and as a result we suffered much distress and frustration. We are both much wiser now and although the experience was painful at the time, we have greatly learned and developed as a result of that pain.

Chapter 7

During the early years of life in our cottage and whilst I was pursuing my psychic interests through books and in circle development work, I always seemed to have at the back of my mind that there was something not quite correct about my fascination for the subject as a whole. Some kind of guilt feeling kept intruding, and eventually I could see that I would have to choose between institutional religion, and the spiritual path I was moving along. I was in truth being offered far more than the dusty old dogmas of the bible, but traditions die hard and the penalty for changing them is guilt. One medium I was seeing during those days picked up this turmoil within me and suggested that I should meet a friend of hers who was an Anglican Vicar at a church in Bournemouth.

I had several meetings with this enlightened man. He was totally tuned into the whole subject of psychic phenomenon and yet somehow managed to fit it into his work as an Anglican Vicar. He understood my predicament perfectly, and went to great pains to assure me that I was not offending any thing, or any one in my quest, and after a full and lengthy discussion he took me into his church and gave me a blessing.

This vicar achieved a great deal for my future spiritual liberation, but it is not everyone who can receive such enlightened treatment from the church. Most people will say that they have not been overly affected by religious education at school, but when invited to add up the hours spent at assembly each week, the formal lessons of Religious Education, and Sunday school, and the religious attitudes of some of the more enthusiastic teachers, the amount of time spent on religious persuasion is very considerable.

I must admit to a certain gratification that our two children, Lisa and Paul, do not seem to suffer from the guilt problems that I used to have when I was their age. I think it is fair to say that any restrictive religious influences that may have affected them during their time at school were balanced by our totally open reactions to any strange experiences they may have had. When I question them as to whether knowledge of the subject of psychic phenomena has been a hindrance or a help, they both assure me that it has underlined the value of their own lives, and helped them cope with the world around them. They both seem to have remembered only vaguely any religious education that they received at school and I assume from this that when I was educated there was more emphasis placed upon the subject.

When Eve first came to the cottage, the children were at Upper School near Wimborne. Paul was aged 15 and Lisa 17. Up to this time we had not told them about the direction our life seemed to be taking. Though we had answered their questions openly and frankly, they were still ignorant about the way our spiritual life was developing. I think I felt the need to protect them from the confusions that were besetting us, for we were barely able to sort out our own questions, and to foist our problems on to the children seemed unfair. However, there comes a time when children reach an age of awareness that cannot be denied, and the time had come to start owning up to what we were about.

Religion was not really something we had ever discussed with the children. We had avoided the subject because of our own uncertainties. We had tried to develop their sense of responsibility, and encouraged them to respect plants and animals and that was about as far as we felt we could go. But now the time of reckoning was upon us and it was going to be difficult.

I was very aware, and so was Brian, that we had a responsibility not to damage our children and this must be the same problem that other parents face when they discover beliefs that are contrary to the old religious dogmas. I suspect that this is a paradox that will create increasing problems as the New Age begins to take effect. On one hand we have the ancient dogma of a religion which demands an unquestioning acceptance of some rather strange beliefs and theories. On the other hand, there is an increasing need to develop the individuality of our children so that they should become capable of resisting the negative influences of an extremely materialist society. At times we wondered if we were on the correct path, but even if we had not been we did not feel that we had the right to cram our beliefs into our children. Their lives belonged to them, and the mere fact that they had been born of Brian and myself did not mean that they had to think as we did. There seems to me little point in going through the process of life if you are expected to be a mirror image of your parents. At the same time it has to be admitted that children look to their parents for guidance. It may be that the best form of guidance that parents can give comes from a discreet blend of honesty and concern.

Somehow we managed to get across to Lisa and Paul that we were trying to find out the truth about religion as such. We told them that we felt that when a person died, they did not in fact go completely. We told them that we knew certain people who could speak to people who had been dead for some time and that such dead people could sometimes help other people living on earth today. They seemed to accept our explanations without trouble, and were neither frightened or perplexed. Indeed they accepted the ideas very lightly, as I suppose young people do, for after all they were far more interested in the world that they knew rather than the one they did not know. In fact they readily admit these days that they used to laugh a little at us, and thought we were sometimes a bit strange.

Paul was not born with the talents of his sister. From the age of two he seemed filled with energy and zest for life. I was told the date and time of his birth and his sex eight months before he arrived, and I was also warned that he would be highly psychic in later life. From the age of five onwards he often said things which seemed far more profound and wise than one expects at that age. He seemed to carry within him certain truths, and I assume that these must have come from a previous life. He has always had a gregarious personality and his perception of life and people has now become quite astute, as have his visual psychic abilities. By this I mean that whereas Brian and I usually *sense* the presence of entities, or beings, or whatever they might be called, Paul would actually *see* them, often with startling clarity.

He is very aware of his own psychic abilites, and has been since about the age fifteen when he first began to see psychic entities. At this stage he kept seeing a lady on the landing and in the bedroom of the cottage. He described her as wearing a long black dress with a long white apron tied with a large bow and with crossing straps. She would just appear and observe him. The first time he saw her he said he was startled, but not frightened. He observed her presence on and off until we actually moved away from the cottage. She never attempted to communicate with him and neither did he with her. I must say here that I was also aware of a similar lady around the children when they were young, especially when they were ill. There came from her a feeling of love and care of children, as though from a nanny or a nurse.

33

As time went by Paul began to see more and more. During the last two years of life at the cottage he saw Roman soldiers on a number of occasions as he worked in the garden. They would just stand around looking at him. He described them as being dressed in red and black skirts with an armour upon the top part of the body attached by black leather straps. They had metal helmets with a red vertical band. We have tried to trace records of this uniform pattern but so far have had no success.

The Lady on the Landing

One winter evening whilst sitting inside the cottage he became aware of such a Roman pulling on his arm and, visually only, he experienced this Roman taking him out into the garden and onto an area of the driveway, where he was joined by more Roman soldiers. They held his arm and made him look into a very deep hole in our driveway. The hole was about 25' deep and 12' × 15' wide. At the bottom was a huge piece of stone. I was in the room as Paul experienced this sensation and I could see that he had become very hot and flushed from the experience. He said that although he was aware of being in our driveway which was surrounded by trees and bushes, the whole area had appeared as being very open without any trees and he could sense some kind of dry stone wall in the field adjacent to the cottage.

It was at about this time that Paul started to experience psychic visions which were unpleasant in that they always involved road accidents. He saw one such accident which he felt sure would involve Brian and he asked Brian not to drive along a certain route for some time. The stretch of road concerned was notorious for accidents and I suspect that what in fact Paul was picking up were etheric emanations of past accidents upon that road and interpreting them to concern his own family. This is a type of psychic experience that Brian's mother has often been dogged with. I told Paul to make a mental request that such experience be taken away from him and I also sent him to speak with Harry Johnson, my psychic development contact who agreed that this was the best thing to do.

However, from time to time Paul has continued to have similar experiences, particularly when he was driving late at night, too fast and too tired. We came to the conclusion that these were warnings for him to slow down and served as a form of protection. One of these incidents was taken up by a psychic contact of mine when he saw Paul, and he was able to elaborate a little further on these experiences. Paul had been driving home one night very late and had felt a great pain in his head,chest and legs which took several hours to go away. Again it appeared to be emanations of a road accident. My psychic friend was able to tell Paul that it was in fact a friend of Paul's who had died in a road accident twelve months prior. He was trying to warn, not Paul, but another friend who knew Paul, to take much greater care when driving. The name of the threatened boy was given and the information was duly passed on to him by Paul.

Today such visions seem to have left Paul, but one evening he described to me seeing what he said was the nearest thing to a fairy he had ever witnessed. I knew from his description that he had seen a nature spirit, part of the Deva or nature kingdom. It was an area of psychic phenomenon of which he had absolutely no knowledge, but I knew it to be a good and pure level of communication, and I was pleased that he appeared to be graduating to higher realms of contact. The vision he experienced was of a small impish like gnome with a mischievous smile on it's face. An absolutely typical garden gnome, except that this was not made of plastic but appeared from a hedge and then disappeared. I beg the reader to be not too eager to scoff. What Paul was seeing was some form of spirit emanation that was connected with plants and trees.

It was necessary for him to sense it in some visible form, so why not a gnome? For that is the traditional form of our garden spirits. When we buy our plastic gnome from the nearest garden nursery, and plant him legs astride and arms a-kimbo beside our plastic pond, are we not recognising, and personifying quite unconsciously, the nature life of our garden? Why else would we put the little man there?

Having read all this my reader might well imagine Paul to be some kind of angelic youth. Not at all. He is very full of life and energy, very into everything a young lad of his age would be – cars, music, girls, holidays and general fun. I think it is terribly important to stress how vital it was, and still is, that this should be so. His psychic powers cannot be denied, and because they are so powerful it is essential that they should be balanced by a healthy enjoyment of this material life. It may be that later in life he will wish to explore the dimensions that are open to him, and indeed use them for the good of others. But right now his problem, and his task, is to come to terms with the physical world and the best way to do that surely, is to enjoy it. Even so, he recognises the potential within himself and is starting to apply it. Other young people seem to be attracted to him. They respect his psychic experiences, about which he is very frank and open, and they accept his advice and counsel if they are troubled.

Lisa has a very different character from Paul. She does not show any signs at this stage of outward psychic abilities. What she does manifest is an ability to read people. I was told at one stage that Lisa, like Paul would make good use of her psychic abilities at a later stage in her life.

She was a very talented child, academically, musically, artistically and athetically. She could have developed any of these talents to a high degree, but turned to her artistic abilities against the advice of her teachers who would have preferred to see her pursue an academic career. From a very early age I sensed that Lisa found outsiders difficult to get on with, so I was particularly interested when William Thomas stated, in one of his sessions, that Lisa had not lived an Earth life for a very considerable time. She had chosen to return in this life as my daughter, a relationship that we had shared in a previous lifetime. Because of the long term she had spent in another dimension she was finding it difficult to adjust to the Earth way-of-life. She found it particularly difficult to come to terms with the insincerity of others. Though I have no statistics to prove it, I suspect that most children who have strong psychic awareness have this powerful inbuilt sense of justice and concern.

Indeed it is evident to a greater or lesser degree in most children. (I would hasten to add that this does not necessarily mean that they are angels!)

We had great difficulty coping with Lisa's complex personality as a child. However, with the help of Brian's family and our own developing awareness I like to think that we gave her useful assistance along the early stages of her life-path. Certainly she considers that our understanding and treatment of her spiritual problems helped her through some very bad times.

There is a strong understanding among psychics today that many souls are returning to Earth for the particular purpose of using their deep inner knowledge to assist their fellow beings through the transition into the Aquarian or New Age (see Chap.17). One cannot but feel concern for such souls launched into our materialist culture, for the guardians of our religious welfare seem to show little understanding of their problem. Theology and spirituality make uneasy bedfellows.

Lisa turned to her artistic abilities for a career and became a natural history illustrator. Paul turned to farming, and as he had a natural ability to work with machinery, he concentrated on mechanized farming and machinery in general.

Family life is never easy. It consists of a mix of personalities all trying to get on together under one roof. In many respects we were no different from any other family. Yet we were different in that Brian and I were upon a path of self exploration, which seemed to be heavily guided and yet was very confusing and unsettling. We had the normal family problems of children growing up and trying to find themselves within the confines of family life and we had the considerable responsibility of being self sufficient and self employed, which in itself limits free time. When you work for yourself you never really ever leave it behind. Our life has been one of extreme hard work both physical and mental. Luckily Brian and I had a driving force and intuition within us which we gradually learned to harness and apply. Everybody has this intuition within them and many of the answers to our modern problems lie in using it. Hopefully this story of ours will encourage others to look for the hidden abilities within themselves which will gradually improve the quality of their own lives and those they come into contact with.

We did have one great advantage that has enabled us to survive the many pressures. We seem to always be in total harmony with each other. We understand from the psychic information that we have received from various sources that we are not strangers to each other in this life time and our union this time was planned, presumably by us. Without the strength of this age old union, I could not have continued to pursue my search for truth and I can only assume I would not have reached the stage at which I am today.

Chapter 8

Before I go on with the main story, there is an apparently superficial but interesting event which I must recall here. One summer evening around the same time as my first meeting with Eve, Brian and Paul and one of our sheepdogs were in the garden at dusk, approximately 9 p.m. Suddenly and most vividly appearing before them all was a pure white goat. However, what was so startling was its position about one foot above the ground level and the silence with which it passed across the garden and through the hedge into the next field, not disturbing the hedging in any way as it did so.

Had Brian and my son been the only ones to see this 'goastly goat', I may not have believed them when they told me. However, what served to convince us that they were not imagining it was the reaction of our sheepdog. He had been most alarmed and fearful of what he could see. He sank down to his haunches and lay low until the goat disappeared. His normal reaction to another animal, be it fox or dog or cat or to a strange human, would have been to rush at it and bark. What he was seeing was obviously abnormal to him and he was ill at ease with the experience and was more than glad to get inside the cottage as soon as possible.

We thought no more of the event other than to tease each other about going into the garden at dusk and running the risk of seeing the 'goastly goat'. I would say that it was not something that worried us and it somehow added a special touch to the ancient cottage and its garden.

However, about six months later, I went to visit an old school friend in London for a few days. During one of our conversations, knowing of my interest in psychic matters, my friend related a piece of information given to her by an acquaintance of hers who was a medium. This lady had described the friendship between us since school days and went on to say that she knew I lived in an old thatched cottage in Dorset and that I kept a beautiful pure white goat in my garden. My friend, knowing this not to be so, remarked that I had two sheepdogs, some cats, rabbits and guinea pigs, but no goat. She would however check this point when she next saw me. As you can imagine, she was more than taken aback when I related to her the tale of the 'goastly goat'.

It is a tribute to the resilience of human nature, should we allow it to be so, that we can look back after only a short time and view a period of trial and tribulation with a certain detachment, even humour. And so, when Brian and I look back on the days when our relationship with William Thomas was developing we recall a rich mix of anxiety, physical exhaustion and lively family activity. We always took time off at the weekends to walk the Dorset countryside, and the cheerful unconcern of the children and our tribe of animals did much to remove the loads from our shoulders. We even had a caravan for a short while which we used to explore further afield. On one such exploration in North Wales, we came across a stone circle marked by a ring of quite small stones. We became quite excited at our find and I remember insisting that the four of us should hold hands and dance around within the circle. I knew next to nothing about stone circles and yet I instinctively sensed the spiritual power or energy that was contained within those stones. We will find ourselves in much closer relationship with stone circles later in my story.

One continuing task that occupied our energies was the renovation of the cottage. This physical labour, though arduous and expensive, also did much to keep our minds in a healthy balance between the realities of the physical and spiritual dimensions. The cottage was a typical old country cottage, built of cob with a thatch roof and with no foundations whatsoever. It literally sat on the earth!

Brian and I and the children put a great deal of ourselves into that cottage and there are many incidents that make us all laugh when we look back on those times. One day we decided to remove the old fireplace in the living room, hoping to discover an old inglenook. No Egyptian tomb was opened with greater care, or more heightened excitement than that aged fireplace. The tension rose as Brian prepared to knock away the last few bricks, and then! A deep rumbling sound and the room was filled with half a ton of rubble and soot, avalanching down from the chimney breast in which it had been pent up maybe a century ago. We just stood there, all four of us, peering blackly at each other through the layers of soot and dust that covered everything. The animals had deserted us with singular alacrity, and were cowering in some remote corner of the garden. But, emerging through the swirling clouds, stood our inglenook! We had no hot water at that time but we managed to clean ourselves up by boiling pots and kettles of water. The dogs, to their great delight, were taken down to the sea for a bathe.

Another of our projects was to build a small extension on to one side of the cottage. This required the usual footings, but the cottage was sitting on top of several springs, which play no small part in the later chapters of this story. Every morning when we went outside to work on the footings they would be full of water. All four of us would be out there bailing away to keep the level of the water down. On one such morning we were most anxious to clear the water completely as we were expecting a visit from the local authority building inspector. During the course of bailing out, Brian dislocated his back and we had to drag him onto the kitchen floor where he remained for some considerable time including the duration of the building inspectors visit. We laugh when we look back at the bizarre situation of the inspector discussing building technicalities with Brian who was prostrate upon the floor. The gentleman showed no sign of emotion whatsoever about holding a conversation with a person in such a unusual position, while the children and I were giggling hysterically in the adjoining room.

At one stage we installed a large log burning boiler to heat the cottage and our water. On the day of installation, the system developed the most terrible airlock and the explosions and crashing from the boiler and its pipes were beyond belief. The children and I were terrified and fled into the garden to join the animals in their now accustomed refuge. For many weeks I wrestled with that boiler, trying to control it before the system finally settled down.

We were always most vigilant when knocking down walls in the cottage to search for items buried deep within the cob, but all we ever found were a few horse shoes placed there by the builder of the cottage for good luck. Because of this, when we filled in areas of wall we placed items into it for somebody to find in the future and in Paul's bedroom we placed a plastic box in the wall full of items relating to the age that we live in. We also left a written note saying that the finder was a lot luckier than we had been in uncovering hidden treasures.

During the winter months, following our first trance communications from the Reverend Thomas, Brian and I came up with the idea that it might be possible to open our garden to the public during the summer months by joining a national gardens organization, which passed proceeds from such openings to charity. We

41

made an application to the organization, the garden was inspected for suitability and was immediately accepted.

Our first opening was on a Sunday afternoon in June of 1985. We were amazed and delighted at the response. We had three hundred and fifty visitors to that garden in just one afternoon. We opened the garden on summer Sundays for several years to follow, always with a very high turn out of visitors, many people returning month after month and year after year. Many, many times people told us of the effect the garden and cottage had upon them. Often they returned with friends to witness the experience. All commented on the peace and the feeling that they had stepped into another world, just by coming up our winding driveway.

Brian and I were very keen to trace the Rev William Thomas to find out who he was, and what place and what period of time he came from. From the statements made by the landed gentleman who spoke following the Reverend Thomas on that first evening, we felt it more than likely that they both hailed from Dorset, probably within the last four hundred years of our cottage's existence.

The Cottage

So we went to Dorchester to trace the church records of Dorset. We found that a Reverend William Thomas had been the rector at a small village near Wimborne from 1576 to 1619. It seemed most likely that this was our communicator, as we could trace no other clergyman of the name of Thomas in Dorset at that time. We also found out some further information about William Thomas from the records which we noted but decided to keep very much to ourselves, in the hope that he would confirm certain points in later communications. We discovered that he had been involved in a court case against the Lord of the Manor of Long Crichel, of which he was Rector in 1579. This was over a disagreement about tithe apportionments. We also discovered that in the year 1736, when William Thomas was no longer alive, the parsonage in which he had once lived had been submerged in a large man made lake when his old village was relocated.

Once we felt that we had probably confirmed the Reverend Thomas's existence, we were more than keen to receive further communication from him in an attempt to gain more information to work upon and worked at trance communication through Eve several times during the following three years. Gradually we obtained a fuller picture of my relationship with this deceased parson and the reasons for the rekindling of it. Tape recordings were kept of all communications received and I will now give some excerpts of material received soon after we had first traced a William Thomas in the county records:–

'It is most pleasant to speak with you once again, to share the pleasure of your small abode, yes the light within is like the light of a very large Christmas tree. The vision from your hearthside can be seen quite a long way my children, steadily we have seen it burn brighter and brighter as the years have flowed. Earlier this evening I heard a conversation about time. I have been aware of each one of you for several years, probably more years than it would be wise to tell you. In the earliest days each one of you resided in different parts of the country. Slowly you have been brought together for a purpose. A purpose planned and decided amongst you before your lifetime upon earth. Take comfort and strength in the future years from the knowledge that you have known each other for much longer than your few earth years.'

I must make mention here that this phenomenon of people coming together, or being brought together for a purpose, seems to be more accepted these days. Dr Arthur Guirdham brought emphasis to it some 30 years ago with his work on Cathar reincarnations.

'You are working quite well now. Following the clues with a great deal of expertise. Then that is to be expected when you have myself guiding you and putting into your minds those thoughts of curiosity that encourage you to leave your work and go and seek. Though the seeking has been hard, it has also been quite exciting has it not madame?

I was never a man to hide myself. I have two firm feet that I stand upon. That was always my way. There was no need for me to hide from those men of little understanding in my time or from the annals of time itself. For I hold the key to a puzzle that was originally more than a small part of my creation. There is still another book for you to find. It is a large heavy book that would be difficult for you to pick up. You will find further information of my legal dealings with the squire.

I understand why you like to find your proofs. I appreciate the honesty of the reasoning and so it is my promise to encourage you in your seeking. Around the time of the full moon within the month of March, so you will find a build-up within your own minds, your instincts will grow stronger my dear. Trust them, for you have been led carefully from month to month and your own capabilities of sensing and seeing have improved. Give yourselves a little longer to delve in your books. Be most careful that in writing you put down each date correctly, for there will be many who search the records and try most hard to bring them to discredit, but stand firm, you have your records, they are the real proof.

There is another one who is needed to guide and help you in those records. He is a gentleman now reaching the age of wisdom, getting a little frail, but with a mind that is sharp and alive and used to searching amongst old manuscripts. Work closely with him. He has those special skills that you require to make doubly sure that your facts are true.

Have you seen the ducks that play among the spires of my small house of God? Often I still walk the same pathways that I did many years ago. This is one of the delights of my newer body. I can now walk where I please and none of the elements of Earth can stay me. You understand?'

It is clear to see that William Thomas is enjoying and also approving of the fact that we are attempting to trace and prove the validity of his existence and his communication. In fact he even

44

directs us in certain areas. He has also now confirmed that he had legal dealings with the Squire and he mentions that ducks now swim above the roof of his once 'small house of God'. We have to assume now that we have found out who William Thomas was and now is.

It is also at this stage that William Thomas starts to indicate my need to develop my own psychic abilities in order to understand and find the 'treasures of the site'. When he talks about 'spirit' I assume he refers to what we call 'soul'. This aspect of our being is receiving much more emphasis in the New Age. He says:–

'Have faith. Remember that those powers do not just belong to you, the young lady who lives on Earth at the moment. They are loaned to you from the greater powers and it is your spirit who is the true custodian. So there is no need for you to have a lack of faith, for it is not you that is the custodian, but your spirit. It is only for you to learn to work with your spirit. That is simple, is it not? It is most natural. I will walk with you and teach you further, for it is my delight. I spend a lot of time with you on this property that makes me feel at peace, for I missed not owning such a property those many years ago. The right of owning was snatched from my hands, and my spirit cannot rest until one or two wrongs are put right. But that is my story and not yours and it is God's story to take from this land that which is his, for the work that is of his choosing. We know that you are deeply respectful of this truth, that is why such a responsibility was placed with you both, a few, years ago when your children were children.'

His concern for material values is interesting; the wrongs of four hundred years ago (using physical time) have still to be corrected. But as my own psychic skills develop, it will be seen that William Thomas' perception of his own situation also develops, and he becomes less and less concerned with the mundane earthly matters of the past.

He goes on to indicate that I have within me the ability to dowse for artifacts beneath the ground (see Chap 17), and I have to admit here that though I realise I could develop this talent I have not made the effort to master it that I should! I keep looking to others to do this sort of work for me. I must also confess that at this stage I still exercised a certain scepticism, and found it all very difficult to believe and accept. I was not totally convinced and was wary of just how deeply involved I was prepared to be. I felt in a way very much on my own and I wanted to protect myself, my sanity and my family from possible disillusionment. I had to learn to have confidence in myself, and as the reader shall find out, I learned the hard way.

Chapter 9

William Thomas had told us in his last communication:–

'There is another one who is needed to guide and help you in those records.'

We did indeed meet such a one who totally fitted the description and it is he who has spent much time searching the historic records for me in order that I could give some substance to this story. In a later communication William Thomas also tells us that there is a very special area of information relating to our land, the details of which will not become known to us until a particular man makes contact with us. In his own words he says:–

'We know that you would wish to unlock time, but the area that you would unlock has a special seal. There is only one who is capable of breaking that seal. The day that he comes here you will find the deeper evidence. We have only been permitted to part with some knowledge of these fact.'

As predicted, that help arrives in due course, but not until we had endured two years of total confusion and had virtually given up all hope of ever solving the mystery of the land upon which we lived.

It was at this time, in the Autumn of 1987, that building and road developments were beginning to appear around the cottage. We had become aware of the cloud on our horizon some six months before and we had received a warning about it from William Thomas. This is what he had to say:-

'The boundary line of the property today is considerably altered from the original habitation. In some respects it should curve outwards into a wider arc. Are you aware of this? I am going back to the original boundaries. Before another moon has come and gone a part of the land will have come under the hammer of the auctioneers. In my day it was quite a simple procedure to sell a parcel of land, but those who sit in judgement in your time are most confusing fellows. They make the most simple thing most complicated.'

We now understood that there had been a change of ownership in the land alongside our cottage. The original owner had sold to a building company who had assumed that they would get building consent. However, a far more alarming situation had also arisen. A local Draft Development Plan had been published for the comments of local residents. Imagine our horror to find that in this Draft Plan, our cottage was completely missing and a new housing estate was in its place.

Brian and I were frantic in our written objections to this future proposal. How could the local planners even consider demolishing such a beautiful old cottage with it's well matured gardens, to replace it with a modern housing estate? But we had a lot to learn! There are many, many people in our society for whom the only purpose in life is to make money. Making money, as such, is not a bad thing. Indeed it is very necessary and can do a lot of good. But when the process is divorced from any spiritual groundbase, it too easily becomes an obscenity.

In reply to our objections, we were told that because we lived upon the fringe of the new housing development, we had the choice to be included in it if we so desired. Many here may say why did we not cash in on the situation and take the opportunity to move on? However, apart from our psychic knowledge of the cottage and its land, we had now spent ten years renovating the cottage. We had a beautiful garden which was now open to the public on a regular basis, and I was now running my own small cottage industry. It did not suit our worldly situation, let alone the spiritual one, to sell off to a characterless housing complex.

So we made it clear to the Local Authority that we did not want to surrender our cottage and I approached the Listing Authority in an attempt to have the cottage listed to protect its future. Sadly this could not be done, as the authority did not consider the property suitable for listing. There had been, they said, too many alterations and additions done to it over the years.

As well as making known our intentions to stay, we also had to raise the question of an ancient public footpath that ran along the driveway of our cottage before leading into an adjoining field. While the cottage remained in a rural setting, we were quite happy that the footpath should run along our drive, but it would become too much of a burden with houses all around us, and many more people using it.

We were assured at this stage that in the event of future housing development, the footpath would be diverted away from the drive. This footpath was to become a major factor in the eventual fate of our cottage. It was a factor which had been foretold long before we had even thought of moving to the cottage. A very elderly pyschic friend of ours who wasn't aware of it's existence, told us that the footpath belonging to the cottage would one day be the 'key to the property'. At the time we had no idea what this was about, but we

Treasure Hunting

never forgot it, and one day it's meaning became only too clear.

The reader will recall that we had been told of 'treasure' that was buried at the cottage. This news had triggered off an energetic search which lasted for almost two years. Many members of the family were dragged into weekends of endless digging of enormous

49

holes which produced absolutely nothing. When we now look back, having since worked alongside experienced archaeologists, our methods seem so obviously crude and inefficient. We certainly found no buried hoard, and from the few artifacts we subsequently found close to the surface, it would seem very likely that if there was anything there we would have missed it in our ignorance and clumsiness.

Anyway, though defeated, we were only a trifle deflated. I decided to approach the British Dowsing Society to try and seek a dowser of archaeology. Looking back now, I realise I should not have been looking to others for help in this direction, however, as I have already stated, I had very little belief in my own psychic abilities at that time.

The British Dowsing Society put us in touch with a highly respected dowser from their organization. I wrote to him to see if he would be interested in dowsing upon our land for possible archaeological artifacts. I gave him absolutely no information about our psychic adventures and as far as he was concerned our reason for asking was because our cottage was very ancient. Mr S. agreed to come and asked for a map or plan of our cottage so that he could 'map dowse' in his own home first. (see Chap 17). This was duly sent.

Imagine our excitment when we received a letter from Mr S. to say that he was amazed to find what he had picked up from his map dowsing. He said it looked as if we had the proceeds of several robberies buried at various points throughout our garden. He said the buried contents included gem stones, church ornaments, gold and silver. We were beside ourselves with wild excitement. I can only laugh when I look back at the state we got ourselves into. Having read the contents of his letter, I was in considerable need of a glass of brandy to calm my emotions. The gentleman requested that he be allowed to come to our cottage in order to carry out actual site dowsing to pin point the areas for us to excavate. Of course we only too willingly agreed and a date was set.

In a very short time he arrived and spent a considerable time dowsing on the site. I must emphasise that Mr S. was, and is, a highly respected member of the Society of Dowsers. He is a well known author with several books on the subject to his credit. He has a wide reputation for sensitive and accurate dowsing. At the end of the afternoon, having had a meal with us, he departed leaving us to start our excavations the following day. We spent hours and hours painstakingly digging and yet again we found absolutely nothing. What was going on?

We made contact and discussed the situation with the dowser. Not only was he most surprised at our failure to uncover anything, he was, as can well be imagined, highly embarrassed. He said that it was possible that the dowsing readings might have been cases of 'remanence'. This means that the objects had been in the ground at one time, but had now been removed, leaving behind indications of the presence which are capable of being picked up through dowsing. However, he said he had already tested for this phenomenon and did not feel it was the case. He also said that as we had a considerable amount of clay within our garden, it was possible that the dowsing readings had become confused, as does sometimes happen when clay is present. At the time of writing, nothing of any great moment has been found, and we have assumed that somewhere along the line a mistake has been made. Nevertheless I do feel that there is something remarkable lying beneath that land which will one day be unearthed.

Brian and I had hoped that the finding of buried treasure would finance the development of a project for a craft centre and open gardens. You will recall that we had planning permission to enlarge my cottage industry but lacked the finance to do so. We also hoped it would serve to rescue us from our now ever worsening business financial situation.

By now I was seriously starting to question the correctness of dabbling in psychic matters. I was also seriously concerned that I had maybe given the children false ideas about spiritual existence and eternal life, and I went through a phase during which I absolutely shut out any psychic influences I may have felt. I studied as many religious teachings I could upon the subject to see if in any way I was transgressing some sort of doctrine, or moral code.

Chapter 10

Our failure to uncover any treasures came as a shock. We had placed far to much faith in our expectations, and had tailored our finances accordingly. Our living style would have to be altered, so we put the cottage on the market.Not only were we distraught, but disillusioned and disillusionment was the one thing I had always feared. It was that fear that was the basis of my reluctance to develop my own psychic abilities. In short, I had no belief in myself.

Brian and I made the decision that we would sell the cottage and move elsewhere, hopefully further into the country to get away from the housing development that was starting to eat into the area of Dorset in which we lived. We had also decided that we would have nothing more to do with psychic matters. We would henceforth live a completely worldly life. Making these brave decisions was one thing, sticking to them was another, for there were influences at work that were not going to let us go that easily.

The cottage went on the market during January 1985 and in the course of the following eight months, I showed sixty prospective buyers around it. All fell in love with the cottage and its garden and yet I received only one offer of purchase and that was too low for us to be able to accept. However, as always we had yet another very successful season of garden openings with record attendances.

By August of that year, we were beginning to get more than a little concerned at our failure to obtain a purchaser for our cottage. We had been out and about ourselves looking for possible new homes and had found one or two that we felt we could move to. Eve, knowing of our frustration, suggested we join with her for further communication with the Reverend William Thomas. We agreed, however, with great reluctance. Our attitude towards William Thomas that evening was hostile and frosty. We felt let down by him, and looked to put the blame for our failures at his feet, not ours. As he began to speak, I felt he was making excuses. I was not prepared that evening to absorb his words or even to attempt to accept his comments on our situation. The atmosphere was heavy and William Thomas was well aware of it. Towards the end of the communication, I made the statement, 'We will move.' And that was our intention at the end of the evening.

I will now give a verbatim report of that evening's communication, but I must first say that although its contents meant very little to me upon that August evening, within one month and following a very strange and moving experience which I had, the communication of that evening was a total revelation to me and ultimately the cause of my change of direction. From it I discovered the reason for which I had come to the cottage. In short, the evening's communication was the most important of any I had received so far. The parson knew me through and through, how could I continue to doubt and reject him?

'It was a great time ago and before the Romans came and desecrated this precious land and before the Saxons wrecked its peace. It was used for a purpose far more divine. It is from this source that you gain these powers. They go back long before your records though. It is of little use to search records this time though, my dear. You did exceedingly well last time. Some areas are still hidden, but they are of little interest. You received the most important information, that I am a person in reality, not a figment of imagination. To know that is a comfort to me, working as I do. For I can send forth information of a different calibre to that which I am used to. I know I can work in a more direct manner, but I am more skilled in manipulation. It is most interesting at times to watch my words flow beneath a pen and to watch the mind working away believing that the words it was forming were it's own.

We know of your continued struggles and of the way you champ at the bit continuously. It has been most frustrating for both of you and I know that there have been many tears shed and many times when your minds and hearts were filled with fear, which has not entirely left you. But from that fear is slowly arising a greater strength and understanding such as you have never had before. It is a cruel lesson and often our hearts cry with you, but we must not interfere. There are little things that we can do, but we have not the right to change the natural order or to stop you treading the paths that you have chosen to tread.

The charge that you received many years ago still sits upon your shoulders. You especially, madam, have not entirely released it, though you have made strong attempts to market your property, deep within you is still a strong hold to the underlying responsibilities of the property. I would say to you that each of the children of earth have two minds and unless both minds work in complete unison, the natural laws of earth will not be obeyed, for the one mind is pulling against the other. Do you understand?'

Me: 'No not completely.'

WT: 'You know that when thoughts are sent forth, they contain within their construction a certain strength and a power of creation. Not all of them will stay with life in them for ever, but some will, and the thoughts that are there, deep within the subconscious mind have a greater strength and power than the thoughts of the surface mind.

If the thoughts of your surface mind, which are closely linked to your problems of earth, do not ride easily with those of your subconscious mind and the passage of the soul, then what you create will be torn in two directions. Often I watch you walking in your garden and searching your heart and your mind for the reason why certain things must be. It is then that I try to draw closer to you to encourage your mind to flow along patterns of understanding. But for quite a long time the shadows have been too strong and I have not been able to gain a close enough entry.

We know that one half of your being longs to obey the laws of your land. We know that orders must be met. I had the same problems when I lived on earth. But still I say to you child, you must want your changes with the strength of two minds before the pattern can change along the ways that you would choose.

You have been puzzled, have you not, as to why no purchasers with their bags of gold have walked towards you. Yes, it is confusing to seek the right explanation. But I say to you, with my hand on my heart, and the other on the holy book, that it is none of our doing. It lies more within your own hearts and the laws of being that are at the deeper level than the laws that your bank manager creates. It is your own hearts and minds and thoughts that have brought these laws into being. I would ask you now for your own goodness and the peace within your own mind, to be truly honest and admit that when you have sought other properties and decided that yes, you would like to have owned them, has there not been deep within you one or two tears when you have come back to the arms of this property.

But maybe you can understand how your own tears and your own deeper longings have brought into being laws that are not

54

created by your government, but by powers of much greater strength and being. In your time you call them metaphysical states of being. Does that sound reasonable to you? But you are puzzled?'

Me: 'I am confused.'

WT: 'That is a healthy sign for you to be confused. It means that now you are beginning to look at the situation from more angles than one. It is a good beginning. If you would truly release yourselves from the responsibilities of this property, you are free to do so and you will have our blessing and our help to enable the business affairs to flow correctly. But first you must once again walk in your garden and face the truth that lies deep within you. Converse with your husband and make final conclusions and give your final answer to your creator together in the privacy of your own bedchamber. That is the world that belongs to the two of you.

You hoped to hear different. I know. I can see it in your mind. But how can we give to you information that is possibly acceptable to you at this moment, but not totally truthful. What is it you do not understand?

You have both been living two lives. The one half of you has been closely involved with the normal responsibilities that a family and the laws of earth bring to you. Only you can truly answer as to whether the both of you have handled your business affairs wisely throughout the past years. We can help in many ways but we can never live your lives for you. We can uplift. We can bring the rays that will make you happier and stronger. We can fill your minds when they are pure with the thoughts that will open doorways to other states of being, but only if you give us the correct recipe.

The other part of your life has worked a certain way and then for quite some time it has stood still and that was not because we made you stand still. That came from yourselves, from your own inner selves, who were trying to manipulate and find answers in wrong directions. So your own spirits, your own subconscious created the blocks which to both of you appeared so frustrating. I do not say pleasing words to you, but words of truth which will take you both forward into a future that is once again expansive. One or two decisions have been made which are healthier than the ones you made earlier in the year. I am correct. Recently you have altered your minds in one or two ways from those opinions you had at the beginning of this year. You have changed your decisions, not ones concerning the property, but personal decisions which have been most beneficial to your peace of mind.

Have you not noticed that recently, although your problems are still heavy there is now a freedom, a shaft of light that is bringing into your minds an awareness of other ways in which you could draw to yourselves the answer to some if not all of your financial problems? (This was so as we had already taken steps to re-mortgage the cottage.)

Do you not agree, or is confusion still there?

Me: 'I am still confused.'

WT: 'Tell me of that confusion.'

Me: 'You gave us information two or three years ago of things to be that have not come true.'

WT: 'You are speaking largely of the trinkets that lie hidden in the soil of this property. They still lie hidden. They are here but it was not for you to find them, was it? Otherwise you would have found them. They are here. They have been here many centuries and they lie quite deep within the soil. It will take some highly experienced people a long time to find them and the main problem for people such as you seeking treasures such as these, is that you have very little practice.

We know that it is most difficult to have dangerous holes on your property. But still I say, that the trinkets are here. We have not told untruths. But they will take a long time to find and experienced hands should organise such a search.

It is a very painstaking task to find tiny objects in a pile of ancient mud. In some of the places the holes would have to go down deeper than you are skilled enough to handle. The natural skills that the daily employment that your husband has gained over the years will give to him the understanding that this piece of land is very different to how it looked two and three thousand years ago. Over the centuries it has developed a depth that is now a fair amount higher than in those days when treasures were buried for safety here. The treasures did not belong to the churches of your time. They were treasures that went back before the Christian churches came into being in this part of the country. So we are talking of considerable changes in the measurements of the land as it is today.

Does that take away a little of your confusion.?'

Me: 'Yes.'

WT: 'But does it bring back more faith in us and what we are trying to do for you?'

Me: 'Yes.'

WT: 'That is good, but your courage is sometimes a little low. Make your choice, the two of you, as to whether you can truly leave this child who has become part of your life. For that is what this property has become. Deep within you, not house and garden but a part of your very being and it is to that you must answer.

Make your decision once and for all and you will find that the waters will once again start to run freely. Instead of me taking from your shoulder the load that has been so hard to carry, it seems that I have placed it even more heavily upon you. But that is not so, we have given to you a little bit of magic that will work, but the two of you alone can use the key that will bring life to this magic.

Do you understand or are you still confused?'

Me: 'We will move!'

WT: 'The decision is made on the surface, now make it deep within your being. From this moment on, if it is your choice to leave the property, then you must truly say farewell, and not fret over what will happen when it loses your protection. It will no longer be your responsibility. Have I made myself clear?

This night I would that I was capable of joining with you in a glass of claret to lift your spirits. A glass of wine was most beneficial to me when I came home tired and weary from the many problems that were brought to me. I cannot give you a tray with wine upon it but would you please imagine that the offering I give you in deep sincerity is as real as the glass of wine I was able to enjoy many years ago when I walked these hills and vales.

I will withdraw from you now feeling a little sad, for I know that your hearts are heavy. You hoped to hear something different, but I ask you once again to realise that although we love you dearly, we can only do so much for you. We cannot take away that which you have created. Whether it be a creation within your daily lives or a creation through the powers of yours spirit. Think kindly of those who work so hard to steer you along the road of enlightenment and the day will come when you will awake and realise that from this period of trouble and anguish you have drawn jewels of much greater worth than those that lay in the soil beneath your feet.

I leave you the blessings of the God Almighty. Farewell.'

For the rest of that month of August, we continued in our attempt to sell our cottage. As I said before, we had not given any great thought to the Reverend William Thomas' last communication with us. We did not like what we had been told that evening, maybe because it was too close to the truth for our own comfort and at that time we were not prepared to admit to our mistakes. Looking back, it is not difficult for us to see now that apart from our financial situation forcing the sale of our cottage, we were almost trying to sell as a gesture of protest; an expression of our disappointment at the way things had turned out. As I have said before, we looked to place the blame for our failings at the Reverend Thomas' feet.

However, an event during the early part of the following month of September served to force first me, and then Brian to look deeper into ourselves for our motives and our true inner feelings about that cottage and its land.

I had gone into the field by the cottage one afternoon, to feed our three horses some hay. I was making a fuss of them as they munched steadily away when suddenly from two fields away there was an eruption of noise from a huge earth excavating machine. I had not seen it there as I went to feed the horses and suddenly it burst into action.

My reaction shocks me even to this day. I fell to the ground sobbing. I felt as if my heart was being torn out. I banged my fists on the ground screaming 'No! no!'. In the middle of this outbreak of torment, I could sense William Thomas saying to me:- 'Go inside the cottage and listen to the recording of what I had to say to you one month ago. Perhaps you will then understand why you feel this extreme pain and emotion as you witness the machine tearing at the ground.'

I flew inside and found the tape recorder. As I listened to William Thomas' words, this time with an open mind, I could only too clearly see that it contained extraordinary wisdom. One part of me, the surface worldly me, was trying to sell and move. Yet deep within, that was not my desire, and the two parts of me were in conflict causing confusion and sorrow. Deep within me this land meant more than I could understand at that time and when I saw it being violated something within me stirred. Somehow I had to find out why I felt this pain and why it meant so much to me.

When Brian came home that evening, we had deep discussions regarding these events and he once again listened to William Thomas' communication. The result was that we decided we just could not leave the land, although why we still did not understand. We had to obey our inner feelings because they were so potent and to disregard them caused too much pain.

This message was the turning point of my life. I now began to understand the complexity and the great power of thought. It was a power that gave us the ability to direct our lives. At last the lights were beginning to shine in the dark castle of my soul. I saw that there was joy ahead for me if I could but continue to listen to myself.

Of course we still had a critical financial position. Nevertheless we decided to take the cottage off the market for the time being and to make every effort to improve our financial situation. Over the following twelve months, we never looked back. We pulled ourselves back from the brink of financial disaster and, as always, our garden continued to draw large numbers of visitors.

Chapter 11

Having learnt a very painful and costly lesson, it was obvious to me now that I would have to try to become more psychically self sufficient. But self confidence is not achieved over night. I felt I really needed more evidence from William Thomas if I was to cement a trust between us and I required something to build that trust upon. Why was this parson, who lived on a Dorset estate so long ago interested in me now?

When William Thomas had first communicated with us in 1983, I had merely listened to what he had to say. I did not feel it right to question him in any way for it seemed somewhat disrespectful. I did not like to appear distrusting, especially of a cleric, be he dead or alive. But I was now beginning to understand that I did not need to 'ask' questions. All that was necessary was for me to 'think' them. So once again I asked Eve to work for us and as always she willingly agreed. Again the results were very good and the communication served to explain several areas within my own memory that had concerned me for years but for which I'd never had a satisfactory explanation. On this occassion I was to find out just why I had been aware of a vicar watching me as a child and why, when I first married, I was visited with faint memories of a grand life style. Here within the following transcript lie the answers. William Thomas starts off by greeting Brian and then turns his remarks towards me :-

'I bid you welcome Sir, it is good to greet a young friend once again. You have had your arms well filled with much mud in the last few months have you not? You have worked on some most difficult sites. It has its benefits I suppose, although I must admit that it is not industry that I would care to partake of so I admire you my young friend for having the courage to stick with such a difficult physical and menial task. The day will come when you will score, have no fear. Though at present it may be a little difficult and your purse strings are pulled tighter than you would like, these days are good for you, they will teach you to be a little more responsible when the jewels of the future once again unfold before you. These difficult days will not last for ever, though you will struggle for some time yet.

(Then, addressing me) I have heard you asking a question. You wanted to know if you were the daughter of the old hag who resided in this cottage. The answer is most definitely not. You belong to the big house, not to the small one. Amongst five daughters could you find yourself. That will give you something else to go searching for. But you are there, sitting in the centre of five girls. You know that once again you will start tearing the garden about and it is good that at long last you are using a measure of practical common sense to work out the difference between measurements of my time and those of your day and age.

The horses still hide secrets beneath their hooves, but unfortunately they are not for you to find. The site they cover up is of such antiquity that I doubt if anybody has the knowledge to recognise what is there any longer. The dolts and fools who would tear up that land can see no further than their eyes and their purse strings can take them. That is their loss and your gain, for still on the boundary lines lies the fringes of a fascinating tale which goes back before the Roman invaders. So I taught in my day, for it was my will and delight to also spend many hours searching ancient records and other avenues which brought to light many secrets of the past. It is those energies that I share with my young friends today. Your stories of the past that I have given to you about the Celts who dwelt hereabouts many centuries ago was real and the evidence lies still in the ground though there is little chance that much of it will ever be found. From time to time possibly one or two small trinkets will float near enough to be found by those who have true inner sight in such matters.

Around your neck at one time lay a strand of wonderous sparkling beads. They fully startled the eyesight with their beauty and with their many sparkling colours as the lights in the ball room played upon them. They lay on a most beautiful milky white neck. In those days you were my favourite, but I never told your sisters for that would not have been right. And so the bond was made which has never been broken.

I continue to be interested in your life from that bond of faith and love that was struck in this county of Dorset so long ago. You wondered why a tale of your property has unfolded so and what part I have played in its history. Now you know. I was already reaching a senior age when you were in the brightness of youth and there was within you, even at that age a special quality which could not be liberated by one lifetime upon earth.'

Needless to say following this communication, I was off once again to search the records. William Thomas had said I had been the middle of five daughters in the family who resided in the estate house when he was the rector. The records showed, as he had said, that there were five daughters. Another point of great interest that I was able to find out from these same records was that this middle daughter had, after marriage, gone to live in Somerset. At a later date, my researcher John took me to visit the estate on which she had lived as a married woman in Somerset. My reader will perhaps remember that upon my first visit to Eve at her flat in Bournemouth, long before any trance communication work was attempted, she had described to me a lady from the past who she said had lived in a country house in Somerset. Eve had said this lady had a strong connection with me. It would now appear that she was picking up upon my past incarnation as Catharine Uvedale of Long Crichel in Dorset, who married into the Preston family of Cricket St Thomas, in Somerset (Chap 13).

I found it all rather astonishing. I could not deny that I had been aware of a clergyman watching over me as a child. I also was well aware now that many children are visually very psychic when young and so that would explain why I could see him then and not now. Also there was no denying that I had been having recollections of a rather grand life style long before I had met Eve. However, there were still some unanswered questions. The main one was my attachment to this piece of land. William Thomas had told Brian and I that we had lived there well over three thousand years prior. He had told me of a life lived nearby some four hundred years ago and I had been able to back up his facts in the local records. I certainly would not be able to prove a life lived three thousand years ago by searching records. Was I to accept this fact without question, merely because I had been able to prove the validity of the other information I had been given?

But I was to receive a second confirmation of the information that related to my life on that site, three thousand years ago. The reader will recall that that in one of our earlier communications from William Thomas, he says:–

'We know that you would unlock time, but the area that you

would unlock has a special seal. There is only one who is capable of breaking that seal. The day that he comes here you will find the deeper evidence, we have only been permitted to part with some knowledge of these factors.'

In January 1986, the healer Cyril, who had helped us with some of the early trance experiments put us in touch with Bob Sephton, a dowser of earth energies. The particular field in which Bob worked was in dowsing for natural energy fields and in many cases rebalancing and readjusting them, particularly for people who were adversely affected by them. As a result of this meeting, Bob was asked by our healer if he would be interested in making some dowsing investigations around the area of our cottage. My reader will have to trust me when I say that our healer gave absolutely no indication whatsover to Bob of the psychic history of our cottage and land. All that Bob was told was that we lived in an old cottage which seemed to show evidence of containing certain energies which attracted and possibly benefitted people.

One evening Bob rang to say that he had been carrying out some map dowsing on the ordnance survey map which covered the area of our cottage. The reader will recall from our experiences with the archaeological dowser, that it is quite normal to dowse from a map before moving on to the site itself. Bob had received some very interesting and unusual results and asked if he might call to see us and discuss his findings and also to carry out some site dowsing. We willingly agreed. The information given to us upon that first meeting with this dowser of earth energies was quite remarkable. Before I elaborate, I should explain that it is possible for a dowser to collect detailed information over the area of his work using a technique of question and answer. He asks a direct question in his mind which receives a 'yes' or 'no' answer. He gets this from the reaction of a pendulum which he is holding. The trained and experienced dowser knows the answers to his questions from the behaviour of the pendulum. Often a dowser will use a rod, or even bent wires in place of a pendulum. But in our case Bob used his pendulum, and from the results he gave us there was no doubt in our minds that here was the 'breaker of seals' referred to by William Thomas.

Bob told us that I had been a priestess on this cottage site in the year 3626 b.c. He went on to explain that Brian and I had both been here and were responsible for setting up a stone circle. We had returned again some 2000 years later, in 1514 B.C., to make adjustments because so many other stone circles were being formed

The Cottage

across the world. The radiations of energy from these circles were beginning to affect one another and there was a need to balance the system. In modern parlance, the grid system had to be rationalized.

The 'circle' around the cottage site consisted, we were told, of seven inner stones, in which the cottage now stood, an outer circle of twenty one stones, and a further outer circle of fourteen stones. Eight of these were 'splitters', six were 'directors' and five were 'spirals'. The centre of the circle was in the hallway of the cottage. We were told the site was female and its purpose was one of evidence. Brian and I had returned to this site in order to make the necessary adjustments because the energy site was not operating correctly. Time was running out for mankind. Energies needed to be rebalanced, and the people prepared for the coming of a new spiritual age (see Chap 17).

There are no stones there now, not that can be seen anyway, but I cannot help wonder if what Paul was shown lying at the bottom of the pit by those Roman soldiers, was not one of the stones of the circle.

As can be imagined, it is not easy to accept blindly the sort of information passed to us by Bob but we had received, over 3 years ago, indications from William Thomas that the site we were on was sacred and was over 3000 years old. He had also implied that Brian and I had been 'familiar with these lands' in antiquity (Chap 6).Surely this dowser had just given us a confirmation, in greater detail this time, of what the Reverend William Thomas had already told us? As I have said, Bob knew nothing of our trance communications and when I told him later about them, he was not really interested. That kind of psychic communications had no appeal or interest for him.

As far as I was concerned this information answered several questions. I could not get out of my mind my reaction that day when the mechancial excavator started it's dreadful work of desecration in the adjoining field. I did indeed have some deep affinity with this piece of land which I could not deny. From the day Brian and I had first come to the cottage, we had felt we had 'come home'. We were continually aware of the 'pull' in our solar plexus' whenever we travelled away from the cottage, and by now even our son was beginning to feel it. And further back, in my childhood, there was that feeling that I was to prepare myself for something that was to be done in the future.

We were now really beginning to understand the depth and complexity of our situation. In many ways it was a great relief to have reached this stage. We had no choice but to accept our circumstances though it was still difficult to surrender ourselves entirely to the intuitions that beset us. It was a particularly interesting situation, for it seemed to emphasise the degree of self-will that was always ours. At any time we were free to ignore the influences that were coming through. Through our experience, our 'knowledge', we had learned to trust in them, to have 'faith'. But there is a world of difference between having faith in what someone else tells you, and what you have learned from within.

How difficult it is for today's citizen to hear that small inner voice. Without it, all we can hear is the cacophony of the modern world, a thousand leaders saying do this, do that, until we decide to move in the direction of the loudest voice instead of the quietest. It is that still small voice which has commanded my increasing respect and attention over the years. I discovered that there was another part of me besides the one that gets on with every day living. It was not as though I had ever had hours to spend day-dreaming for I have always lived a very busy and active life,and yet within every day there would be some time when my mind would roam into distant realms of thought, and time spent in this inner land was always totally engaging and satisfying.

Bob told us that adjustments were necessary, the land energy needed rebalancing. We asked if he would do that for us and he agreed. He was without doubt the person to carry out such an operation. We had been told of his coming and had to assume there was some far distant connection between him and us. I must emphasise here that apart from his natural dowsing abilities and knowledge in his particular field of dowsing, he was also, as a scientist and engineer working in the energy industry, particularly well equipped to work out the complicated calculations required to re-balance the site. I fear I am not qualified to explain in any detail what exactly he did. Actual dowsing was not the only skill involved. It took several months of calculations and preparations and an awful lot of paper. It involved not only our cottage but several of the well known sacred/energy sites in Dorset. The correct month, day and time were set for the reintroduction of the energy to the rebalanced site around the time of the New Moon and a small ceremony of dedication was held. Our site was now in perfect balance and in total harmony with other similar sites. We had, as far as we could see, completed what we had set out to do within this lifetime. In many ways it felt a great relief. If we achieved nothing else upon this land, we had left it rebalanced for ongoing time and to the greater benefit of humanity.

I have to admit that I was at first somewhat bemused by the principle of 'site rebalancing'. But as so often happens when working in the psychic field, I started to come across other reports of incidents which all seemed to point in the same direction, and emphasise the attention and effort that is being given to 'energy sites' today. This area of work was totally beyond the capabilities that Brian and I had developed within this lifetime. However, we had by trial and error, and not a little guidance, arrived at the right place at the right time in order to find the right person to effect the right adjustments. We were flattered, even a little awed that we had been given such a task. Now that it was done we felt a joyful, if slightly apprehensive, anticipation. What next?

Chapter 12

As I now move towards the next part of my story of life in the cottage, the reader will find us yet again having to come to terms with deeper realities than those we were accustomed to. What we thought would be necessary or desirable to us in our worldly life did not actually apply from our inner or spiritual point of view. The conflict between material desires and inner wisdom can produce some very painful lessons, but the rewards lie in increased strength and confidence, and an ever developing understanding. The way to achievement lies in letting go, and reaching out for the future. There is no such thing as the present, only the past and the future. If you can't look forward to each day, you must look back, and to look back as Lot's wife found out, is to become a pillar of salt, not much use to anybody.

During this period of growth I received much practical help and encouragement as I started to develop my own skills of psychic communication, and it is the story of this development that forms the next part of my tale.

It is difficult to ignore the strange coincidences of fate that bring like minded souls together. I know that in my case it is often more than coincidence, it is the gentle prodding of intuitive forces that I receive more and more clearly as the years go by. Some people appear to be closed to those influences, and yet they appear in my orbit, so to speak, and play an important part in the development of my life. It may, one day, amuse the idle curiosity of a researcher to explore the hidden impulses that bring such meetings about.

By 1987 Brian and I had reached the stage of classing our friends and acquaintances as those who knew the 'real' us, and those who knew only the 'worldly' us. It was a strange situation and difficult to handle at times. To make what were apparently worldly decisions only after consulting our inner knowledge produced actions and behaviour which sometimes seemed a bit strange to those friends who were not in the know.

We wanted to tell our closer friends, and did sometimes try, but after a few unsuccessful attempts we gave up. We had taken a long time to reach a level of knowledge and understanding which could not be explained in a few minutes. They were politely attentive, but we could feel that their credulity had been stretched beyond the bounds of friendship. We were either daft, very naive, or on some ego trip. One or two of them were prepared to concede that there might be something in it, as we seemed to be in all other respects quite normal. But sadly they were wrong even there, for we were not normal. We were leading a double life all the time, and were longing to 'come out'. Even among the group of psychic friends and mediums with whom we were associating we felt awkward and restricted. We needed to mix with people with wider interests, with people who not only had their heads in the clouds, but their feet firmly on the ground. We needed some sort of intellectual link with our spirituality. And so the next move was set up for us.

Ronnie Skerman, a friend I had made through my craft connections, told me of a house in her village where rather interesting meetings were held each month. She went on to describe how speakers at these meetings dealt with a wide variety of subjects, ranging from say, crystal healing to early Christian philosophy. They covered any area which was usually avoided by our society and from which useful knowledge and ideas could be drawn. It was part of a much wider group called the Wessex Research Group which organised these activities throughout the six counties that covered the ancient kingdom of Wessex.

I was more than interested in what Ronnie had to tell me, for it seemed that at last we might meet up with people whose interest in the New Age stemmed not only from psychic experience but also from intellectual interest. Even so it took me a while to muster the courage to tell Ronnie that I was not merely interested in such things myself, but heavily involved. After all it's not so long ago that such a confession would have brought the hysterical accusation of witchery, with it's inevitable slow death by drowning or burning!

It was through the W.R.G. that I met, as predicted by William Thomas, my researcher. After long service in the Marine Commandos, John Lloyd had retired to become a schoolmaster in a Dorset primary school. He has spent hours and hours over the past three years researching and processing transcripts of tape recorded communications in an attempt to get some order into the events that have occurred. I owe a great deal to this now good friend of ours, for it was the encouragement and support I received from him during this time that kept me going forward when at times I felt very much like stopping. And it was through him that I managed to widen my circle of sympathetic acquaintances into intellectual and academic areas.

The Wessex Research Group see themselves thus:–

'A co-ordinating network and focus for groups and individuals concerned with new areas of research and experience. We are interested in spiritual, cultural, artistic, historical, ecological and scientific fields. We operate in the belief that there is enormous potential within many people for growth of consciousness, but this is often stultified by the feeling of being alone in their quest, and the active fellowship of like-minded seekers will give them both courage and new areas of search.'

Over the last three years I have attended many meetings and lectures held by this organization. At long last I was not alone and I could now relate my experiences to people who understood and were interested. Following one particular lecture at John's house I made contact with the speaker, as I could see he was 'tuned' into an area of experience similar to mine. This was Harry Johnson, who kindly wrote the foreword to this book. I outlined the situation to him and asked if he could help me. He willingly agreed and spent many hours helping me to break down the barriers of my culture to gain the confidence which would enable me to communicate with William Thomas myself.

However, before I elaborate on this, I must tell of events of a more worldly nature that were creeping up on our horizon. The housing development around our cottage was now becoming far more of a reality. The land adjoining ours had changed ownership more than once and full planning consent for housing and roadway construction was imminent.

One early summers day in 1987, Eve was having tea with me in the garden when she announced that the Colonel who had once lived in the cottage and who had been the first one to communicate with us through Eve, was warning me that when development commenced, we were going to experience tremendous problems because of the presence of underground water. We were already aware that there were springs in the area, and it is an interesting point that most of the religious sites of antiquity are involved with springs; this being particularly evident in the ancient history of Wessex.

Brian and I gave thought to the Colonel's warning. I had myself heard of cases where old cob cottages, which had no foundations, were badly affected by spring water which had been diverted by new buildings. In view of this and in view of the planning permission soon to be granted, I wrote to advise the Planning authority of the nature of the construction of our cottage and the proximity of all the springs. I pointed out that we had depended upon a surrounding field ditching system to control the water over the years and asked that they should pay great attention to future drainage to protect our ancient cottage and it's well known garden, which was still drawing large numbers of visitors. I also reminded the them that it was necessary to divert the footpath from our driveway. My letters were acknowledged and I was assured that all would be taken care of.

We were very saddened at the thought of all that beautiful farm land around our cottage being eaten up by development, and we had had great dreams of owning and extending the gardens and starting up a craft venture. But such dreams were now becoming more and more remote. It was going to be very difficult to live with the changing environment around our home, particularly as we now knew the land alongside our garden was also within the bounds of ancient stone circles. We could not bear to imagine this ancient site being built upon but could see no way of preventing it. I could make no public announcement about the site because nobody would have believed me. Perhaps if we had been able to uncover some worthwhile ancient structure or artifacts, I may have been able to find the courage to be more outspoken.

It was at this point that I started to work with Harry to develop confidence in my own psychic abilities, for I could now see that I was responsible for working out my own problems. It had also become clear that if I was to be able to listen to my intuitions, to spiritual guidance, to that still small voice that some call God, then I needed help in clearing away an awful lot of mental rubbish that had built up over the years. Preconception, illusion, delusion, prejudice, and belief, mostly collected from other people, are like locked doors through which the mind struggles to hear the muffled voice of truth on the other side.

I was first asked by Harry if I had ever felt like writing down any of the psychic influences I had felt. I told him that I had thought about it but had not followed it up. He then told me that I should try this as a possible method of communication. The best time for me to be receptive to this type of writing was in the early hours of the morning, after having slept for a few hours. My physical body would then be refreshed and relaxed, my mind would

The Wendy House

be uncluttered with the events of the past day and not yet involved
in the day to come. He suggested that perhaps I should set my
alarm for 3'oclock in the morning.

The method I finally adopted was to make a mental note upon
retiring. I would not then be startled from sleep by an alarm clock
but would awake when I was ready, and when I was required to
do so, that is if there was communication for me to write down.
The result was dramatic. For several nights I awoke in the early
hours feeling wide awake and tremendously hot, which is most
unusual for me as I am by nature a chilly mortal, most dependent
upon wooly clothes and hot water bottles. Also I sleep like a log
always and it is very seldom that I wake during a night's sleep.
Initially, I was reluctant to rise for I admit to being a little frightened at that stage. However, the waking and heat sensation continued to occur and so I decided I could no longer deny these
promptings.

I left my bed at 3 o'clock, went downstairs, took a pen and pad
and sat in an arm chair. At the same time I played music quietly
upon headphones because I love music and I find it a very good

way of disconnecting myself from my immediate surroundings. I sat and waited, rather frightened, as I was expecting the pen to dash across the paper as in the case of automatic writing. Automatic writing is a form of communication where the medium will sit with pen in hand, more often than not with her eyes closed, and the hand will write, uncontrolled by the medium. The speed at which the written word appears upon the paper is usually unnaturally fast, often presented without punctuation. The content of the communication is passed directly from the guide or communicant to the hand of the medium. I daresay the principle is closely related to dowsing, in which the hands of the operator appear to react to some independent force. However, this was not to be the mode for me. After about fifteen minutes of quiet music with my body gently relaxing, I was aware of a flow of words within my mind. I decided to start to write what I felt aware of. The words flowed and my pen wrote at great speed, my eyes felt almost closed, I was writing by feel as opposed to vision.

Much of this early written communication contained instructions and encouragement from William Thomas, directed towards me as 'trainee' communicator. The most marked, almost physical sensation that I experienced whilst attempting to write in this way was that of an immense love being directed towards me. The depth of feeling I received from my guide was almost impossible to put into words. It was a feeling I was able to return after a short while. It is to be compared to that of a joining together of souls. It was, and still is a truly beautiful experience and I now find it difficult to understand why I should ever have been afraid of what I was attempting.

Before I give a sample of some of this early material, I must tell of some information given to me by William Thomas through my writing, which at a later date I had confirmed with another medium. William Thomas had told me that I had been the mother of my daughter in a previous lifetime more than one thousand years ago. He said we had entered into the same relationhsip again during this incarnation for a specific reason. In 1988, about twelve months after learning this, I visited another medium, Mrs P., whom I had never seen before. I travelled a considerable distance away from home to see her. Not only did I tell her absolutely nothing about myself, but I gave her a false name and address. My reason for consulting her was that despite all the direct communication I was receiving, I always had self doubts about my situation. I am not a gullible person and have to be convinced totally before I accept. I think that William Thomas was sometimes a little impatient with this attitude, but in view of my strange experiences, I think this might not be a bad quality to have.

The first statement Mrs P. made to me was that I was a writer. I made little comment, saying that I was really a florist. Again she insisted that I was writing a book. She told me the book was not fiction but fact and said that when the book was published, it would sell a great number of copies and that it would be most appreciated by the American market. She then went on to tell me that when I wrote, my hand was overshadowed by that of an elderly, scholarly gentleman who had been departed from this world for a considerable time. Two or three years prior, William Thomas had promised me that he would make himself known through another medium in order to prove himself to me.

Mrs P. then said that I would require an illustrator for my book, but that I would not have to look far because my own daughter was an illustrator. Then she told me that I had been the mother of my daughter many years prior and that we were back on earth today as mother and daughter for a specific reason. I was told that I would go on to write other books after the first one was published and that my daughter would illustrate them all. At the end of this meeting Mrs P. told me that my own Father, who had now been dead for three years, was standing beside me with his brother, urging me to press ahead with my book. Her description of my father, his brother and their relationship with each other whilst alive was remarkably accurate, as was her account of their interest in all matters psychic when they were alive.

Mrs P. had not met my daughter, Lisa, and would certainly not have known that she had completed her four years of art education in the spring of 1986. In the autumn of that year she had met and married David, an army officer, and at the same time had started freelance art illustration.

Lisa's relationship with David when he was her boyfriend was, as can be expected, beset with the problems of trying to explain to him what we were all about. She had not really been deeply involved with anybody before and so this became a problem that we all had to face for the first time. What to do when an outsider joined our family on a permanent basis? Paul, who was now eighteen had not got us into this kind of situation for he was very much at the stage of loving them and leaving them. He was far more gregarious than Lisa and had no intention of sacrificing his freedom yet. For Lisa it was different. I could not ever have imagined her having lots of boyfriends. We did our best to tell Lisa's fiancee that we had a great interest in psychic matters and that is where we left it for the time being. Either we or Lisa would have to cope with the problems as they occured. At least we had been honest.

So now I write, and of course the illustration both on the front cover and throughout are by the hand of my daughter.

Chapter 13

Here are some extracts from the communications of the Reverend William Thomas as received during my 'free' writing sessions. The passages are drawn from several longer pieces of writing. Some of what he says appears to be of a personal nature, but I have included it here for who is to know what is personal, and what is universal? It seems to me that the opening sentences have a certain poignancy. All my life, William Thomas had been waiting and watching over me. Now at last he can get through to me, and express his feelings directly.

'The pen is mightier than the sword. God be with you. It was I who taught you your love of music. I am still here with you, I can see you clearly. I am here by your side now. Give me time, we will show you how to communicate. Think you of that house, I was there with you and sat and talked so much with you in that lovely garden. There, they came and played the music for us. Not as you hear it today. It is good for your soul, did you not know?

One day the ability was yours, but not in this lifetime. Yes it was the piano, hours and hours of practice. Often it was your punishment for a wrong deed! Music is good for your soul. This is not as you expected. You will get so used to my touch. Listen to your soul, your great strength is there. Yes you will understand what you write, you feel me in your mind. Don't look back at the page, keep your mind empty, we shall learn, my dear friend, back together again, by your side so much. The door is a little open these days. I will instruct your thoughts. You must act with a clear mind. We shall remember together the past. The garden, remember the lessons, hedges, tall hedges and the lawn. Warm days and the perfume of flowers. Don't doubt, relax your mind. I am not a figment of your imagination.'

'Your determination will serve to inspire others. Many will come and speak with you because of the story you tell. Be careful here. Always instruct your listeners to find life's answers for themselves. Yours is a different situation you understand. There has been a great need for communication. Tell people how to sit quietly and listen to their own souls. How to disconnect themselves from the pleasures of the world as they see it today. So many search in their minds. Whilst you live on earth, I can pass to you information gathered at a higher level. Gathered from many years. So many errors I made in my lifetime as a man of the cloth. Many men of the cloth today make the same mistakes as I have done. The love of our creator is all-embracing. There are no boundaries or barriers.'

'The burden is heavy I know, but you chose a life of service and you so wanted to make amends for the past wrongs. You made a promise to me, and I will help you keep that promise. You will return this site to its creator and leave it in trust for the future. Leave it in the hands of guardians, way into the future.

All are interlinked for a reason. No life is pure chance. The pattern of creation is a complex situation. Many work at all levels to achieve a correct balance. Much goes astray. Only those who would be true to their own souls will not wander from the straight track. People of earth are not true and honest to themselves. They do as others would have them do. This is a major fault of the human race and has been for aeons of time. It is hard for the person of poverty to look further than the next meal, and help to them is of the greatest importance. They must be given hope and they must pass this hope on to their offspring. What can life on earth be if there is no hope or foresight.'

'You are a willing channel, we can achieve a specialised line of communication through you. We can pass through you many ideas for a refreshed outlook and a way of life for others. Religion, as such, has failed. A true philosophy for life must take its place. It will occur over a great period of time. Small beginnings.'

'Music is of great importance to the masses today. Much can be achieved through music. Mans mind can be greatly influenced by music initiated through the right mind. The modern composer has a great power within his mind. Many are composers in this time for that reason. People are drawn to listen, yet they do not understand the deeper meaning. This is very true of the young. They spend their lives locked into their music. Much is of great use to them. One day Catherine , I shall speak through you, but you need help and training from those of understanding. Others will speak through you. Seek the help of others. You are a willing channel for a particular type of communication.'

(I find it intriguing that he should use my 16th century name!).

'You grow now in confidence. You begin now to trust again. Seek us more often. Train yourself. There are so many who would communicate with the willing. We can open so many doors for so many. Such wealth of knowledge to share with man of earth. Our two worlds should be as one.'

'Far too much heartbreak is concerned around the death of the physical. Death is but growth, rebirth. For many, in a life of blindness, it comes as a great relief. But so many here would be far more at peace if they could see that those who are left behind have a greater understanding. Grieving families greatly retard the progress of the reborn soul. In fact it can cause a total standstill.'

This last wisdom was confirmed by an incident some two months after the death of my father in 1986. I had gone to receive healing from a friend of mine. During the course of the healing I became mentally aware of my father. He had died of cancer at the age of 75, but I saw him fit and robust, about 45 years old. I had not fully recovered from his death, and he spoke to me quite angrily, telling me to stop visualising him upon his death bed. He said he was feeling fit and well and that I was retarding his progress by remembering him as being in poor health. I happily accepted his reprimand, and I now feel myself drawn near to him quite often.

I once lost a dear friend from cancer. Six months later I started feeling fear, isolation, and waves of pain. I suddenly realised that I was being 'got at' by this friend, and this was her way of telling me that she was dialling my number, so to speak. I then mentally acknowledged her presence, the sensations disappeared and I received a mental message from her regarding her son. She was worried about him, and felt that those around him were not understanding the reasons for his present behaviour. I was able to pass the message on to her daughter. I have been aware of my friend a number of times since then, but the sensations, which were very brief, never returned, for which I am thankful for they were not particularly pleasant. I have already mentioned Paul's pain caused by somebody else's car crash. It seems to me that this initial sensation is quite often used as a summons by whoever wishes to make contact.

Now, back to William Thomas:

'You think, Catherine, of animals and you are correct in your

77

thought. Mankind carries a tremendous karmic debt to the animal kingdom. Farming and the slaughter of animals is handled badly. Movement must be made to re-educate and to put compassion into what is to a certain degree necessary. Methods are very wrong. It does not have to be so. Mankind will have to think again along new lines and re-approach the problem from a humanitarian viewpoint. Do all you can my child, but this is too vast a subject for you to be able to concern yourself with at great length in this lifetime. You will be given the opportunity to work in these fields when you leave this earth. Much can be achieved when you join us again. You will bring with you that desire to work in those realms.'

'You worry too much at the fulfillment of each day. Time is for ever and nothing is ever wasted. All is experience and all is necessary to grow. Time spent in thought is all expansive and if you did not give readily of these amounts of time, then our communication would be impossible. As you would learn another language, so you must learn another discipline. Life is not really of the physical, it should be also and greatly so, of the development of the mind. Much is still so possible through the extension of the mind. You are growing in your mind my child. Just beginning to experience the power of the great emotion that is at your finger tips. This is an energy which you are all part of. Use it. We are all one in the thought form.'

'We shall speak tonight about the senses. You have, I know, felt a surge of energy through your senses have you not? Visual, audible, mental, memory, intuition, all are recharged. Before, they were only partially used. This is true of the people of earth with some exceptions. But with so many blinds drawn, life's experience is in itself limited. Expansion of the mind by discipline is all enhancing. The great need of sleep is in itself incorrect. Refreshment of the physical body can be achieved in far shorter time scales by the successful release of the mind from the physical body. Heightened sensitivity is the correct aim in such experiences. Barriers can be pushed back and potential increased.'

'The atmosphere of your environment is dense with the energies of the past. Sensitives can read from these, but human interpretation is limited and poor in most cases. Depth of communication takes time and needfully so. You would find it most strange to walk one day and fly another. Give time for your wings to grow strong. Worry not at the need for solitude for our thoughts. Write of the experience. Others can benefit.'

'In the correct hands and with profound and wise guidance the young mind can be freed and liberated from a lifetime of

78

frustration. Modern day mechanical devices are a great hindrance to the young mind. There is no substitute for question and answer. Mothers should educate their offspring, not leave it to others. This is a serious, damaging and retarding state of affairs. But to rectify the system a mass awareness of the true potential of earthly life is essential.'

'Times of stillness are of great importance. To unwind the physical body and free the mind are essential to inner peace and development. The belief that satisfaction and progress can only be achieved by frenzied physical exertion in the pursuit of worldly riches is a serious misconception. This state of affairs brings little inner peace, only a shallow and worldly feeling of satisfaction. It has achieved little for the soul. It is, therefore, absolutely essentials to attain harmony and balance between physical life and growth, and spiritual health and growth. The achieving and maintaining of the perfect state of balance brings automatically with it physical health, allowing every atom of the body structure to find its own point of balance. Therefore, an important area in any young child's development is the training of quiet sitting and peaceful surroundings. A story read to a young child, or the encouragement given to the hearing of the sound of music would help to nurture this need and desire for peace of mind within every waking day. Children should be trained and have it explained to them that this is as essential to their bodily health as their times of rest and sleep. Let them observe how an animal, in its natural state, takes a required rest throughout the twenty four hour cycle.'

'Training is always advantageous at these early stages and also in the case of adults wishing to rekindle an inner peace within group situations. Isolation and loneliness are then removed. Only the more advanced student should seek solitude for such continual development. This then is today's theme, the necessity to kindle peace and the running down of the physical system during the waking hours. The greatest benefit within this practice is achieved when the physical body is itself not tired and not in requirement of sleep. Music is the most beneficial aid to this state of peace. This is not time wasted. It is of greater importance to the living being than any physical or material achievement. It is a returning to the root fundamentals of human existence. You must not feel guilt at such times. It is a totally desirous situation. Cultivate and develop such practice so that we may achieve great things for the benefit of mankind. Develop this discipline and observe the physical life drop into its planned order.'

'The energies within the areas of Wessex are powerful. They

have their purpose to fulfil. Great undercurrents are rejuvenating, and expanding. Their absorbance within the population has a desired effect. The theme of mass reality is difficult to explain in worldly terms at present. The depth of worldly reality is little understood. All life is linked into an energy growth and natural balance. You are a small fish in a great ocean of on going emotion, one infinitesmal part of the whole. See child the humbleness of your existence. I shall expand when you wish to give of your mind totally. Train yourself, I can teach and explain at great depth given the right facility.'

'Creativity is in every man. Look to this aspect in the young child and there you will find the foundation upon which to encourage growth of the mind in that young life. Academic faculties will develop naturally throughout education alongside the growth of normal human intellect. However, all academic study can be a very shallow experience if in the inner person, the creative faculty is not also developed. Life without this personal achievement of inner importance will seem almost worthless to countless numbers, causing apathy and a need for escapism, with its resultant dangers.'

'Life is sacred. Every life is of the utmost importance. Too many are brought up under the shadow of repression, feeding into self doubt, self loathing and lack of worth. One generation hands these misconceptions on to another. We require a revolution in our idea of reality. But fear not for the impossibility of these events, for the necessary minds are entering your world for this sole purpose. Enlightened entities who bring with them an inner knowledge for application in the modern world. Entities of great presence are among you today. Many are waiting their time to follow through upon the next level. The wisely and totally taught young mind grows to a wise and healthy young adult and into a fruitful follow through of years. A potential of life is then realised and a steadily improving universal situation results. Small cogs in the great wheel of existence. What hope I am able to speak of. What pleasure for those who are close to despair at the state of the world today!'

I have mentioned earlier in these pages that I had experienced indistinct memories of a life style more opulent and gracious than anything I have experienced in this existence, and my long suffering husband must surely have been irked by my frequent references to a standard of living far beyond anything that we could reach in our suburban semi-detached, or our estate house at Poole. In truth I could not account for this faint but persistent 'far memory' of mine until William Thomas told me of my previous existence as the middle of five daughters at the 'big house'. It was his complaint of bitter law battles that brought us to connect him with the Uvedale family in Hutchin's History of Dorset, for there we found that Sir Henry Uvedale had indeed had five daughters (and six sons) and at the centre of that five was Catharine.

The Uvedales of Long Crichel, near Wimborne, were one of the great landed families of Dorset in the 16th century. The network of the family extended through Hampshire, Dorset and Somerset and the court rolls of these counties contain frequent references to numerous law suits, chancery affidavits and contested wills which seem to indicate that the relations between the various branches of the family were often strained.

My father, Sir Henry Uvedale (if the reader will pardon the presumption) was no exception to this practice and it is interesting to note that in 1579 he was engaged in dispute with one William Thomas, rector of the parish, concerning the income that derived from the great tythes of the manor of Long Crichel, sometimes called Little Crichel. Uvedale won, and the injustice of the battle still rankled William four centuries later. This is presumably the law suit that he refers to in his communications with me, and some students of psychic studies may be sufficiently intrigued to ponder on whether William Thomas's early materialist utterances were deliberate clues to lead us to search in the right direction. Others might conclude that during the early days of his renewed contact with me, his one time pupil, the material aspects of his earthly life still seemed to take up much of his concern. In which case it is only later, maybe, as he begins to realise the difference between his reality and mine that his priorities become more spiritual, or esoteric.

The Prestons of Somerset had their seat at Cricket St Thomas in Somerset and were closely related to the Uvedales. My husband and kinsman Christopher Preston was also executor of my father's will, and is mentioned in connection with a number of law contests after Sir Henry's death in 1599. It would seem that even in those days the energy of the law trundled ponderously onward, long after the demise of the life that employed it! The estates and lands and a few local memories still remain at Long Crichel and Cricket St Thomas but sadly the big houses were both burned down and replaced, so my own memories of casement windows, lawns and terraces must remain as fuzzy reminders of a far life.

Chapter 14

After three months of written communication with William Thomas, Harry suggested that he could help me try to experiment with other methods of contact. By now it was not necessary for me to get up in the early hours of the morning to take writing. I could do it at any time, provided I could relax properly. Sometimes I would actively seek contact with William Thomas and at other times I would just feel the need to sit down and listen, for I felt he had something to say. Harry's suggestion was that I should attempt possible regression work through deep meditation combined with some direct voice mediumship.

I produced a considerable amount of material from these experiments, using deep meditation to achieve a point of contact and yet maintain a measure of self control. Some of the sessions were very lengthy and all were recorded. Once I had achieved a relaxed state, Harry would begin to question me as to what I was sensing. Each time we attempted this experiment I seemed to adopt the personality, or the reality, of some entity from the past. I do not think these entities had any personal connection with myself. Their connection was with the site and my observations were objective, viewing them, as it were, from a distance.

In our first session I appeared to be in an area so far back in time that the earth had absolutely no resemblance to that of today. It just seemed to be all space, and communication between entities was by thought form. I then passed to the time of the setting up of stone circles in which it appeared that the huge stones were moved by the power of thought. Many people will find this difficult to accept and I must admit that I myself had reservations at first, but I have now come to understand and accept many things which at first puzzled me. I seemed to be among a large group of people who had been involved with the setting up and marking of such power sites across the world. I was getting indications that many of us were back on earth again in the present day to work upon the rebalancing of these ancient sites. At this point I seemed to be aware that some of those original people were missing and we were trying to contact them to encourage them to rejoin us again to help us complete the task of rebalancing.

As each session went by, I moved further and further towards present times. I appeared on one occasion to be a Roman potter who had worked near to the actual site of the cottage at Wimborne and could describe a rather shabby working environment, make-shift buildings made of timber and skins and everwhere seeming to be very muddy. I will give here a condensed version of what I told Harry while I was in trance.

'I worked with other potters making produce for every day use. The surplus, of which there was quite a lot, was taken down to the sea on long two wheel trailers pulled by animals. My particular job was the making of tall vessels for carrying liquids. We built great fires in holes in the ground in which we put the vessels, packing the soil around them. We decorated the more important items, those destined for the hierarchy, but the more basic stuff for every day use was left plain. It was reddy brown in colour. I learned my trade from my father, as a young boy. I was not brought up in these parts but was brought here from across the sea, from much warmer lands. I did not die here. We went back to the sea but in a different direction, coming back to this land, not too far away. I did not like the sea journeys. There was not much to eat, you got very dirty and everyone was packed in like animals. But I was a craftsman and I had to go where the need was. My pottery is still lying around, scattered everywhere. There are some unbroken pots lying where we buried our firing kilns, deep down.

We dug the clay from all around here. The reddy clay came from further away, about a mile. There was some here that was paler. The wood came to us on trailers. It was not very good. It was green all the year round and burned too fiercely. It gave us problems. We had to suffocate it.

There were other crafts here. Men worked with leather, making shoes, ropes and equipment for the animals. Metal was very short. All we could do was repair it. We were very self sufficient. What was not here you had to improvise, but most things were well catered for. There was food. We had animals but we lacked fresh grown crops. We had to rely on the peoples in the country around us. Sometimes we had to take it. We were not very welcome. We were intruders. We were spreading our power. My name was Anton.'

At another time I was a Roman who seemed to be in charge of a type of outpost away from the main camp. I spoke of coming to the site and setting up a settlement there. I said that we had found stone on the site and so had made use of it to construct our settlement, combining it with timber which was scarce as it was all down at the bottom of the hill where the main camp was. I seemed to be aware that the site had been the 'magic spot' of the inhabitants before us. I spoke of a large stone slab being erected for the sacrifice of animals as a gift to the Gods. I told of people coming up from the camp at the bottom of the hill to throw gifts at the foot of this altar or sacrifice stone as offerings to the Gods in the hope of gaining their protection. Then I spoke of the dishonesty of some of the soldiers, of how they stole some of the offerings meant for the Gods. I was troubled because we had stolen from the Gods, but I had turned a blind eye to what I saw taking place. When the time came for a mass exodus from the site, hundreds of men, women and children and animals moved out and we could not keep all the stolen items upon our beings, so we had buried them deep in the ground. I was sure that they were still there and wanted to be believed in this because I felt extreme guilt about what we had done. I said that the reason the ground did not drain well here was because there was a large amount of stone buried beneath the clay and that was also where the valuables had been buried.

At the time of these sessions I was aware of the past history of the area in which we lived. The strong Roman connections had been well researched by local archaeologists. I am aware that I am asking the reader to take a lot on trust, however it is an intriguing prospect that some of what I have written has not yet been proved. Should discoveries in the area of the cottage reveal the existence of a Roman outpost or industrial settlement, then it will be that much more difficult for the doubting ones to reject my tale.

What we do know is that at the foot of the high ground which contains our ancient site, with it's powerful springs, there once lay a large wooden walled fortress containing half of Vespasian's 2nd Augustan Legion, about 3000 men. This camp guarded the crossing of the River Stour near Wimborne, and we may assume that the other half of the legion were inland dealing with the tribal strong points at Badbury Rings, Hod Hill and all the other hill forts that threatened the Roman movement on Dorchester and further West.

At one time I appeared to be a little man living in our cottage

84

with his wife in what felt like Victorian times. The cottage seemed to be rather shabby with pale brown external walls instead of the bright white of the present time. The thatch was grey and tatty. Inside it was dark, with few home comforts and only bare boards in the bedroom above. This was reached by a stairway which was so basic it was little more than a ladder. The man was balding and both he and his wife were short. Their children had grown up and left them. I followed the old lady up these stairs into a bedroom which contained a bed on bare floorboards. A brown cloth or blanket covered the bed. Suddenly I found myself in the bed in the process of giving birth! Harry, sensing my discomfort, urged me forward in time, and I found myself outside talking to the little man about the items he had uncovered in the soil whilst working the land. There were no hedges containing the garden as in the present time and I could see across a rough vegetable patch to the adjoining fields.

I strongly feel that this little man was the same who was described by the development circle. He was dressed in very rough clothes and was wearing a brimmed hat. I have the impression that he was from the Victorian era. He gave me details of the landowner at that time, describing the direction in which he had to walk and the time it took him to reach the estate house. Either he, or I, had difficulty in pronouncing the name of the landowner, only the initial sound 'A' (as in acorn) kept coming out. In fact what was probably happening was that it was I who was having the difficulty, as the name was strange to me and I did not then have the confidence to accept any strange words that were coming through. Anyway John checked the records and found that the cottage had belonged to an estate nearby, owned by one 'Willett Lawrence Adye' early in the 19th century. This little man also told me how he had uncovered valuable items in the soil of the cottage grounds as he worked the land, that he had been afraid of somebody finding them in his possession and had, therefore, reburied them.

William Thomas spoke on several occasions, although getting speech from him felt difficult. He gave a considerable description of his life and times. On one occasion Catherine, my previous existence, even spoke through me. All this material felt to me a little vague, however. I was only attempting mediumship at a level of deep meditation and I was not in a trance state. In truth I did not always feel totally confident that the material coming through had not been tainted by my own personality. My trouble coping with Willett Adye's name was a case in point.

I did not find it easy to accept any form of total takeover and so found it very difficult to let go completely. Subsequently I moved back towards 'inspired writing' as a means of contact with William Thomas for I felt this method agreed with my inner feelings. In one of his earlier communications through Eve, William Thomas had himself said :–

'I know I can work in a more direct manner, but I am more skilled in manipulation. It is most interesting at times to watch my words flow beneath a pen and to watch a mind working away believing they were it's words when I know they were mine.' I understood from this statement that William Thomas also is more comfortable with written inspiration. At a much later date when I did again make a further attempt for direct voice contact from him, I sensed his presence, but he did not want to speak and I could feel him willing me to find pen and paper and to put aside the tape recorder.

Here are some of the results from those later writings:–
'It is not easy to speak when the chosen mode is that of the pen. Our link has been that of telepathy. The mechanism used for a direct voice communication is a total take over of the personality but this is only a possibility when the medium used has an intellect that is prepared to surrender to that of another. Some will only link in a telepathic sense, the reason being that the mind of the medium prefers and in fact insists on working in unison – a totally shared experience with neither one of the communicators taking total control of the other. Two minds blending and working together as opposed to a total surrender.

'If two minds are well linked and well matched, in harmony with each other, then in many respects it is a more truthful and fulfilling mode of communication from both the point of view of the medium and the so called communicator. This is a very natural method of open mind seeking and influence. It is very safe and suitable for teaching to an initiate. It is not wise to advocate opening oneself to a total take over. It is not a bad thing for the human intellect to remain and feel in control, even though the results are affected by the influence of the human. Much of that influence can in fact come from the aeons of stored knowledge and experience from past lifetimes. You should not always consider that all influence is external.'

'Have I not said that all should be taught to look inward. The human mind is a great storehouse of knowledge and information taken from lifetime after lifetime of experience. In regression therapy a subject is regressed within one lifetime. All are capable of regressing way beyond the point of commencement of one lifetime. In the training of the young initiate therefore, teach regression of thought towards origins. It is not at all necessary to train towards take over. Look not to exterior means to seek one's answers in life. We must train each to find their knowledge from within. Many turn to external mediums for their answers. Have I not advocated accepting responsibility for oneself?'

'To teach for our New Age Experience is to train everyone to be their own deep source of encouragement and fountain of knowledge. Look not all the time to external teachers.'

'The trained open mind, in so opening the gate, becomes receptive to the life force fountain of knowledge. All knowledge is out there to be reached out for. All are equal and all have equal right to draw upon that fountain of knowledge.'

'I teach and advocate total self sufficiency. By self sufficiency I mean opening up the mind and intellect to inspiration and teaching from the universal fountain of knowledge.'

'There can never be a time when all will be psychic receivers, but all can learn to work from the inside to the outside and not just to operate via external stimulation. All are psychic- most are dormant through lack of use and training. Where do we start? With the very young. Encourage and train that imagination. The most important teachers are the teachers of the infants as they leave their mother's arms. Music, painting and physical endeavour are of equal importance to matters academic.'

It is interesting to note the stress that William Thomas lays on the interplay between the minds of the medium and the communicator. It is not unusual for a medium to appear to relay accurate information and messages, and then to slip into a different style or mode, almost imperceptibly. Those who seek the help of mediums should always be aware of this weakness. What happens is that the balance of minds of which William Thomas speaks has become out of true, and the personality of the medium has started to take over the conversation, so to speak. The medium may be quite unaware of this at first, and then become so used to it that the communication becomes settled into a corrupt form without any conscious intent on the part of the medium. This is why William Thomas lays such stress on the importance of 'do-it-yourself' mediumship.

Over the period of years that William Thomas has been communicating with me I have sensed a considerable change within his approach. In the early days he seemed quite dogmatic in his statements but as time passed on, he has pushed me more and more to act for myself. It was as if he was trying to show me that I had as much ability to seek out my path, as a result of drawing upon past lifetimes of experience, as he did. He has taught me great self dependency and self respect and this is surely his message for all humanity. We all have great potential within if only we seek to draw upon it.

I was beginning to feel by now very much more at home in my communications with him. I was confident that there was someone to reach out to for total unbiased help, someone who would encourage and show me the way to help myself and others who might be interested. William Thomas tells us that everybody has the equal right to draw upon the 'life force fountain of knowledge'. My own experience shows me that this is very true, and I feel very strongly how important it is in this age that everyone, through education and all the other channels of our culture, should be encouraged to seek and to explore, to do everything they can to broaden the horizons of their minds.

Everybody at some time questions the point of their lives, especially today when everything is so worldly and materialistic. We tend to measure ourselves by what we have or don't have. But we are all equal in inner possibility and if we were more concerned with 'being' rather than 'having' how much more joy and peace we would find.

Some will find it easy to ridicule my story, especially those who have been brought up in strict religious beliefs. Anticipating such scorn, it occured to me that it would be easier and more peaceful if I kept my experiences to myself. But William Thomas has helped me see that the whole point of our lives is that they are not only part of our own development, right through into the far far future, but the development of all around us. Loneliness and the pain of sickness, for example, may not appear to benefit the patient in any obvious way, but most people will appreciate how understanding and love grow from looking after someone who is seriously ill. And likewise the patient should allow those around to help and assist in overcoming the illness. There is no great virtue in bearing pain alone, if someone wishes to share it with you.

In short, our experience is our life. Biographies and tales of travel allow us to experience and learn much from the lives of those who have gone before us. They save us having to do the whole thing ourselves. We can live, vicariously as it were, the lives of many other people through their books and memoirs. With the help of other people it becomes easier for us to find our own way. It is my great hope that this book will provide a light for many who might otherwise feel lost.

Chapter 15

As the months passed we gradually realized that the housing estate that was going up around us was beginning to affect the quality of our life. The quiet and peace of the countryside was to be no longer ours and painful as the experience would be, we would have to consider leaving our cottage. It is not difficult to imagine that this would be a very traumatic undertaking. Not only did the situation of the cottage and its garden mean so much to us but we also had a far deeper and long term attachment to the site. In early days we had moved to it by intuition, sensing our attachment to the ancient ground. Now we had been made only too well aware of the reasons, and the ties between now and the past had grown strong. But the past is a mirror for the future. The eye should not rest upon the glass, but pass through it to the landscapes beyond.

Accepting the inevitable and leaving the cottage was not easy. Indeed it was to be the most difficult time of our life to date, and I hope we shall never have to live through such times again. One day, when our anguish was at its height, Eve rang to tell us that she was in touch with William Thomas, even as she spoke on the phone. She told me that she was receiving a description from him of the next home we were going to move to. He described a house, old but not as old as our cottage, that was being sold off from the edge of an estate. He said it was set in twenty five acres of ground.

Meanwhile the water condition in the soil around us was getting worse and worse. The developers started to construct a roadway one hundred yards from our garden. As the autumn of 1987 approached, heavy rain caused the springs around us to erupt, and the roadway construction seemed to send all the water towards us. The fields directly adjoining our garden became totally waterlogged, as they had never been in the fifteen years we had lived there. In the adjoining field which we had tried to purchase earlier, we could see three springs bubbling out upon the surface of the ground. In the end we had to resort to legal action in order to get the developers to admit to the chaos they had created. As a result, they dug a moat along two sides of our garden to cut off the water that by now had made the garden feel like a loaded bath sponge. We were very worried about the damage all this water must be doing to our cottage. It seemed that the warnings from the long dead colonel were well founded.

As if all this were not enough, it was then found that the ancient right of way in our driveway could not be diverted after all. They could find no satisfactory alternative route and our driveway would have to be turned into a public path to the adjoining housing estate. It was like living through a nightmare. Our driveway was long, winding and beautifully landscaped as an integral part of our garden. We could not bear to think of surrendering it to tarmac and fences.

Some may think that we should have taken legal action in our fight against encroachment. But we had already spent a great deal on legal fees during the winter months, battling against the water problems, and even then we had only achieved short term drainage ditches and no long term solution to our problems. We were fighting a very wealthy multi-national building consortium with limitless funds, and planning authorities who seemed to have distanced themselves from our plight.

We felt trapped. Nobody in their right mind would have wanted to stay and it would have been useless to attempt to sell the property to anyone else with all its problems and uncertainties. We had no option but to try and escape. Our three beautiful horses had already been boarded out at a local farm. Our only choice was to ask the local authority to have the cottage and its garden and driveway incorporated within the new housing development as was their original intention some five years prior. By now the unsatisfactory situation was obvious even to them, so they agreed and asked the developers to make us an offer for the cottage. The developers refused, saying that our situation was not their responsibility.

The mental and physical strain was now starting to take its toll. It was bad enough having to leave, but now we were actually having to beg to have the cottage and its garden destroyed. Words cannot describe the pain endured, or the mental battles within.

One evening, feeling desperate, I wrote a letter to the directors of the development company. The letter came from the heart and I begged them to review our position from a humanitarian point of view. They were in a position to give us our freedom and I appealed to them to do so. They agreed to reconsider and following weeks of delicate and painful negotiations, we finally settled on a sale figure. At last we could afford to move.

The Lytchgate

During this time of great trauma, there was, however, one bright spot. As the developers carried out their roadway construction, their excavations uncovered a Roman military road, the course of which ran through the field next to our garden. Eve had told us we were on an ancient travelling route. We had never guessed just how close, and it now seemed more than likely that the news of artifacts and 'trinkets' lying beneath the surface were true, though it was likely that they were at a deep level. But artifacts and trinkets, even treasures, did not seem important any more. We now understood our relationship with the land. The energy site had been rebalanced for the approaching Aquarian Age, and we had to assume that we had achieved all we had come there to do. What had been balanced in the physical, had been balanced in the etheric dimension. The rebalancing of the site, with the emanations of all that had happened on and around it had been recorded, and nothing could erase them.

Some notes on energy, and energy sites are included in Chapter

17. However many readers may still have difficulty understanding the principles involved, and to those I would say that the fact that you are reading this book means that at least you are curious and desire to broaden your horizon. That is a valuable gift in itself. As the years go by, your understanding will broaden and you will be surprised that you ever had difficulties with the new Aquarian dimensions.

I will now give some examples of the writings received from William Thomas as we struggled through this most difficult of times. To make such a decision to abandon the site required much soul searching, and William Thomas gave me all the assistance he could, whilst leaving the final decision to us. Though some of his remarks are addressed to me personally, I have included them here as they are also relevant, in one way or another, to everyone :–

Control of our own Destiny.
'You have a right to choose your pathway from here. There is always more than one pathway. To take one in place of another must not be considered a mistake. The choice of a new path brings with it many more pathways. You yourself have a point of contact as a result of your experiences here. These contacts will continue. An ability is growing. ˆAll experience is worth your attention. *We are the masters of our own destiny.* Yet lack of faith in that ability causes hesitation and retards progress.'

Responsibility for Personal Development.
'Freedom is your entitlement. Move forward in your search of the self. Examine your mind today. If space and peace are what your inner being desires, then seek that path for that is where you will best experience that inner growth.'

'No experience is ever wasted. It is part of the learning process, equipping your intellect for the tasks ahead.'

'Follow those strong inner desires. The days of uncertainty and dependence on others have been left far behind. You know now that you need look to no man for your path in this lifetime.'

'We owe nothing to any man. No human should be chained to another human, or to events. If your forward expansion is not to the detriment of others, then feel free. Your responsibilities to others must be closely examined. Let not any man lean on the shoulder of another and restrict his progress. Does he not then deny the right of that person to grow unhindered?'

Coping with Reality

'It is the growth of your being that is of the utmost importance. The use of your mental energy is far more expansive than the use of your physical energy. You live in the world of *physical* reality today and the restrictions of this reality limit your potential. You need not remain chained. You are as free as a bird if that is what you desire to be. Growth and expansion are your right. Breaking down the barriers of convention are a difficult process for a human life to undertake. Regimentation of life, environment, age, all these restrict the free spirit.'

'You now have in your mind a desired route for this lifetime. That of breaking down the barriers between physical reality and spiritual reality. You have been given much evidence, and now have the confidence to continue the exploration. Build upon these foundations. Doors will always open if you wish them to open. '

The Continuity of Life

'Your experiences and your writings will serve as a spark to countless others. They will help others to push back their own barriers of reality. Life is not a shallow vessel, but an immense continuum, beyond much human comprehension. Many so called wise men have been men of shallow vision, forcing their archaic ideas on the so-called less wise. An animal of the wild has more wisdom than such men. All life is an open ended experience. There is no ending. It is only part of the chain of a continuum. *Look not for a conclusion before you start* for it will not come, not at the end of your present lifetime. Surely you must know that!'

'You yourself have achieved much within the confines of this physical life. It is a touching ground for future growth in other lives. Are you not very different to the person that first entered these lands a few years ago? Have not those years had a profound effect, not only upon you, but upon your whole family and selected friends? Then consider these years as a planned and necessary stopping off place, a stage in your development.'

Children, and the Quality of Life.

'Every child must be taught to understand that his mind is the equal of all who stand around him. No man is less or more important than another, for we all have within us the formula for perfection. Sadly, however, we are very often wrongly programmed from the outset. Kindle enlightenment in the right to quality of existence. This right extends of course to every living entity, be it plant, man or animal. Human life is not for the purpose of domination but for

94

the purpose of co-existence. Nurture in the young child a care for plants and animal life. Teaching today distorts the mind, it is virtually useless.'

Chapter 16

I am today writing this book from the magnificient peace of our new home. However our cottage has still not been demolished and we still wonder if when they excavate that site, they will uncover anything of archaeological interest. For myself, I think it very likely that there is something of great interest lying beneath the soil of that Dorset hill. We are told that it is the site of several springs, wells, and stone circles. We have the plan of a number of very ancient structures as charted by two dowsers in separate exercises. We have psychic evidence not only through myself, but through other mediums, of activities and personalities inhabiting the site in past times and we have had persistent reports of treasures or 'trinkets'. It is an intriguing thought that someone may confirm that part of the story after this book is published!

In the middle of all the anguish of releasing ourselves from our cottage, Brian one day said he had found just the right home for us advertised in a local Dorset paper. On a June day in 1988, he took me to see it. Just one look and we both knew it was right and just as William Thomas had told us, it was old, but not as old as our cottage, it was being sold off from a small estate and it was set in twenty five acres.

How we actually came to be in a position to buy it is a miracle in itself in these days of frantic house buying and gazumping. Many people were wanting to buy it, many had made far higher offers for it than we could afford. However, the owners who were selling off this small farm from their estate were more concerned about who would be coming to live on it than the amount of money they could obtain for it. All prospective purchasers were interviewed and we were chosen. We moved here on the 1st October, 1988. I am now deep in Dorset. The ground is beautifully undulating, we have a river nearby with water meadows, the views are magnificient

The Farm

and the tranquility undisturbed. We consider ourselves truly
blessed after all the anxious times we have been through.

We did bring with us here one magnificient bonus, for we
managed to rescue ten huge lorry loads of that beautiful cottage
garden, from the smallest plant to the largest of trees. It was a very
painful process taking apart the garden that had taken us so many
years to build up, but it felt the proper thing to do. It was a major
physical undertaking but it was very successful and as the Spring
of 1989 approaches, it is clear to see that the greater majority of
the plant life which was lifted from our cottage garden has survived
and is getting ready to burst into life in its new environment.

We can see that it is possible to do here all that we wanted to do
so much at the cottage. This time we have the land, several fine
out-buildings and the years ahead of us. We are in no great rush.
There are in Wessex a number of 'holistic' centres devoted to the
philosophies of the Aquarian Age. Organic farming, psychic and
spiritual development and the many arts of healing are but some
of the studies at the hearts of such centres. Only a few years ago
such activity would have been considered 'crank', or eccentric. But
the few are now the many, and growing in numbers all the time.
It is our hope that the farm will help the growth of this spiritual
age in some similar way. We already have three craft workshops
hired out and working and soon we hope to start a Wessex Research
Group branch where people can come to learn about healing, and
dowsing, and energy and all the other subjects that are opening up
in this Aquarian Age.

97

I must clarify two points which I feel are relevant. I was told by one psychic friend, as I relate earlier in this book, that the footpath at the cottage was the 'key to the property'. Having rebalanced the place, our task so to speak was done. All the visual psychic activity which my son in particular had seen, started to fade after we had made a firm decision to leave. Week by week the signs and the 'feel' of presence faded. By the time we had left the house the area was virtually devoid of all psychic presence. But we were still attached, as it were, and found it very difficult to accept the next stage, and leave. It was the the issue of the footpath that eventually made us decide to leave. It was in a way the release mechanism or key for our departure, and the signal for me to go ahead and write my story. At the time of writing the little cottage lies empty and derelict, a tragic and forlorn spectacle.

William Thomas is still very much with me, a firm stanchion in this strange life that seems to be my lot. His wisdom and guidance are hard to fault. This may sound somewhat presumptuous, but some guides are not particularly helped by those they are trying to help. A totally unquestioning, almost worshipping approach to every syllable uttered by a guide does no good to either party. It was only when Harry took me in hand that, in a way, he took William Thomas in hand as well. Both of us were making mistakes, myself in an area which was completely strange to me, William Thomas in treating the mature grandmother of the 20th century as his young and attractive pupil of the 16th century.

I would like to close with a few more extracts from his writings. I suspect there will be many more to come :-

'I aspire to write great things to smoothe the waters of these troubled times. I can teach mankind to energize themselves to cope with worldwide problems that are today manifesting themselves. Famine, flood and disease are all here to serve their allotted purpose. They are the learning ground of human perception. We are what we create and we can turn the tide of change if we so believe.'

'There is a group of highly evolved souls. You would understand them to be guardians or watchers who look over mankind and the environment. Their influence is among your world leaders today. There are people in high office today who elected so to be and this is because they are receptive to the influence of these guardians.'

'All can aspire to the guiding influence providing they do not adhere to inbuilt dogmas. An uninhibited search for the truth is the only clear course towards such unity of purpose between man of earth and the thought powers of other realms.'

'I have spoken before about musicians, artist and writers. Because of the receptiveness of the artistic mind, they are very often magnificient channels for receiving influence from higher realms of thought. The work of these human souls can then pass through their work to others who are less receptive to such influence. Look to your artists for the light to life.'

'Cast aside old mind patterns, remove all limits, dogmas and creeds. Become as free as was the earliest of earth's inhabitants. You are all energy. Your mind is your most dynamic piece of equipment'.

'Life upon earth is a gift and a challenge. When the numbers increase among mankind who understand their reason for being here, then shall there start to show great improvements in the worldwide situations. It is important, therefore, that we make every effort to light the spark within as many as we can possibly reach in one person's lifetime. Spread the word, pass all I can give you to others. Other communicating minds are doing the same, this you are aware of. You and I are but a pair among so many. We all have our part to play in our particular area of authority. Some by their very nature have to work in a subtle way, others with more flamboyant personalities can achieve more dynamic results. However, both approaches are of equal importance because different people are of course affected by different modes of approach. Some are not impressed by sensationalism, while for others this is the only way to dent their walls of rigid thought.'

'Growth as a human is a learning of the inner self. We are all capable of solving our problems, both internal and external by looking deep within our very beings. The human form is unique and developed to be totally self sufficient and self rejuvenating if only we give it the space, time and peace so to do. We turn too much to artificial aids to support human life and in so doing cut off and deem useless the body's built in abilities. We must instruct the human race to rekindle those abilities so powerful within our predecessors. Time was when there were no artificial aids, then man was truly self sufficient in body and mind. Because of the total lack of self dependence today, man feels inadequate and cannot relate to the reality he has to endure. Escape routes are searched for, despair is most prevalent today.'

'There is insufficient time for peace and self appraisal with the hustle of so called modern high-tech life today. Don't surrender your intellect to machines, they are without souls. Man must interrelate with his fellow man. Personal relationships, giving *and* taking, are such an important part of regaining some natural balance. Just as the animal and plant kingdom inter-relate and should, if left uninterfered with by man, survive and rejuvenate and rebalance, then so should any man who is not engrossed in external stimulation.'

And a final word to me on mediumship, which will apply to many others:-

'You have had contact with many mediums over the years. Because of the necessity, the quality you have received on the whole has been of a higher standard. However, you are only too well aware that even at that high standard, you have suffered much pain and confusion as a result of misinterpretation and it was not until you learned this lesson and made the effort to work on a psychic level for yourself that the path began to straighten for you.

The moral then is that people must be their own psychic mediums and not look to others. No human should place their life decisions in the hands of another. Life is a precious gift and not to be taken lightly. It is irresponsible to use ones mediumistic abilities to influence another persons life. If one human is aware of his mediumistic abilities, then he should use them to help others to dig deep within themselves for their own.

Thank you.'

Chapter 17

Our arrival at the cottage signalled a gear shift, so to speak, in the movement of our lives. We had come into close contact with energies which up till then had been working quietly in the background. The direction of events became more precise and purposeful, and looking back I notice one particular phenomenon of those times. In coming to terms with the events recorded in this book, we often had to turn for help to people who would normally expect payments for the skills and advice that we received. But, apart from the normal services of lawyers or estate agents, we were never asked for money and received instead unstinted help and support which was quite freely given. Other people have remarked that this often seems to be the rule rather than the exception. It is as though there is an atmosphere of sympathy and 'oneness', in which the main aim of like minded souls is to help others to move 'closer in'. It is also noticeable that when money becomes the over-riding factor, when for instance mediums and healers and evangelical 'media' preachers expect great profits from the exercise of their talents, events tend to turn sour, and suspicion and disillusionment become the order of the day. In short, those affairs of man which are conducted without some form of spiritual base will cause pain or sorrow to someone.

This chapter includes a number of passages written by some of those who have helped me through my experiences. The subjects are chosen to help those who are only recently beginning to explore new dimensions. Though touched upon in the previous chapters, they are treated rather more fully here.

THE AQUARIAN AGE: by John Lloyd

In 25 years of service with the Royal Marines, John has seen action in many of the world's trouble spots. He retired in 1971 to qualify as a teacher at Exeter University. It was here that he first became interested in the conflict between religion and mankind's ability to 'think'. For the next 14 years he taught at Primary schools in Devon and Dorset. He is now retired having, he says, learnt more from children than he ever taught them, and lives in Dorset where he lectures and writes for the Wessex Research Group.

Spiritual thinking today recognises that we are moving out of an epoch or age in which dependence upon God, be he called Zeus, Deus, Allah or Shiva, has been the driving force behind the major cultures of the world. It is not that man has necessarily got it wrong. It would be more accurate to say that Man is growing up and is beginning to see his situation more objectively. The age which is in the process of passing is called the Age of Pisces. The one which is now just starting is called the Age of Aquarius, or the New Age. These are but names which describe our intellectual and spiritual progress.

The Aquarian Age describes the beginning of a period of time in which man is beginning to move away from the idea of a single external God, towards the realisation that he, himself, is part of the divine process.

The Aquarian Age is not a sect, cult, or religion as such. It does however contain powerful religious undercurrents which the Churches would do well to harness. It is essentially a movement which through its literature and 'cells' is developing a number of common perceptions. There are no rules, no doctrine, no organisation as such. An intuition is in the process of evolving and it is loosely based around the following statements, which are as close as anyone will get to a common declaration. These are:–

a. Knowledge or understanding of what many call God is gained through an understanding of ones own Self. This ancient Christian truth does not, as some critics claim, lead to egocentricity or self-centredness, but to a realisation of empathy and involvement with all being.

This 'holistic' awareness of the New Age finds that the feeling of 'oneness' is essentially an expression of 'love'.

It is therefore entirely natural that concern for this planet, and its myriad energy patterns we call life, expresses a spiritual responsibility. This responsibility is of much greater relevance than that of personal salvation which is the core of the present Christian doctrine.

b. The emerging talents of healing and dowsing, and the interest in whole foods and alternative medicines are widely respected as New Age or Holistic phenomena. They are seen as symptons of spirituality.

c. Reincarnation is widely regarded as a feasible and likely alternative to the 'one time only' of church doctrine. The evidence for reincarnation is very strong, and the impulse it gives to persoanl spirituality in one plane, and personal responsibility in the other is very great.

d. The Aquarian Age is greatly influenced by certain elements of oriental religion. In particular the concept of dualism, or Yin and Yang. Accepted by early Christians, but condemned by later doctrine, it is seen as a realistic explanation of the paradox of good and evil. If we persist in treating evil as a seperate entity, we will never come to terms with it. Likewise the principles of Masculinity and Femininity are seen as vital paradoxes that have to be accepted and harnessed.

e. The principle of security and comfort upon which the church places such heavy emphasis is questionable. This develops a powerful tendency to resist questioning and doubt which is alien to the spirit of the Aquarian Age. The desire to stand still is detrimental to Man's ability to cope with the modern world. Lot's wife should be left behind, and we should move on with her husband.

f. Many of the old myth figures are being re-invoked, not as deities, but as symbols of profound truths. Even Jesus is seen, not as a deified hero, but as an inspiration and example. In short, the value of the myth is being restored as a tool for spiritual, educational, and psychological insight.

Most, if not all the philosophies described above, come not from theological debate, but from a slow build up of strong psychic and intuitive processes of which this book is a small part. These are being experienced by large numbers of people who are now evolving into the Aquarian Age. Many of them are barely aware of the phenomenon of which they are part. Yet by their actions and talents they are easily recognised.

It is no accident that the guide in this book, William Thomas, lays such emphasis on educational principles. The physical situation of the New Age presents a sombre picture indeed. Pressures of overpopulation, allied to bombardment by super-efficient media are exerting enormous influences on the young peoples of this planet. In England at least, the old established and traditional principles of education are not sufficient to arm our youth against the trials to come. The proof lies no further than the headlines of today's newpapers. Our attitudes to education in the Aquarian Age will require drastic revision. One can only hope that this book will play at least some part in bringing about that change.

DOWSING AND EARTH ENERGIES: by Bob Sephton.

'Dowsing' is the use of the human body to pick up information from whatever is being examined and to interpreting the information so obtained. The greater the 'need' (as opposed to 'want') the more accurate the answer obtained. The human body is a very sensitive instrument and capable of picking up the smallest of energies, be they electrical, gravitational or other types. The dowser tunes-in to what he wishes to assess, not unlike tuning a radio receiver, but he does it mentally. As a result of his thought questioning, some form of minute muscle movement takes place. This can result in the hazel rod twisting, the pendulum rotating or rods held in his hand moving. These various devices are just acting as indicators from which the dowser is able to ascertain a yes or no answer, or the direction in which something might be located. He has to ask a very precise question, hence some knowledge of the subject greatly assists in obtaining accurate answers.

My first attempts at dowsing were an utter failure. I tried a pair of angle rods and they just waved around, so I threw them away and envied those who could dowse.

It wasn't until some years later that whilst on holiday my wife bought me a little book called 'Discovering Dowsing and Divining'. When we returned home I read part of the book and tried to dowse again. To my astonishment I found I could do it, though only in a rudimentary way.

During the earlier stages of my dowsing and after I had reached a certain standard, I became aware that this was something precious which should not be abused. It is a skill in which one is reaching out and upwards in order to progress and become more proficient. One's own ideas and thoughts have to be put aside in order not to influence the answer. Except for teaching newcomers, where obviously there is a need for them to learn and see proof of their endeavours, one does not use it for frivolous activities and the like.

I found that learning to dowse is like learning to ride a bicycle. Whilst we can be shown what to do, the actual art is only achieved by doing it oneself, and by developing one's own particular skill and method. No two dowsers work in exactly the same way. For example when one dowser is using a pendulum, the 'yes' answer to his question may be the pendulum rotating in a clockwise direction, whilst for another dowser it may go anticlockwise.

Most people have the capability to dowse and each dowser develops his own skills and methods, which may not suit another. It is a skill which is self acquired once one has been taught the rudiments. It can take several years of work and experience to reach a professional status, by which time one has probably specialised in a particular field. There is a need for dowsing at every level in many fields, be it medical, health, food, water, minerals, agriculture, to name but a few. I was drawn to earth energies, a subject which I find fascinating.

Generally speaking, dowsing signals will give you three results to a question asked; yes, no, or no change. For example, when I ask a question, my rods swing inwards for 'yes', and outwards for 'no', but if they do not change direction then I must find out why by further questioning. The secret lies in the questioning; ask a wooly question, get a wooly answer!

My background in electrical engineering has enabled me to see similarities between conventional electrical energies, and earth energies.

These earth energies can be difficult to understand, for people are not yet used to the idea that there are forces at work which do not obey the usual laws of science, as we know it today. It is probably sufficient, for the time being, to accept that as a loop of wire carries electrical energy to a table lamp, so earth energy is carried to and from 'energy sites' in the earth. The lines that carry this energy are more commonly called Ley lines, and they can be traced by dowsers. A network of Ley lines covers this planet, on the surface and beneath the surface. When they get disturbed they can exert an adverse or negative influence on people who live near them. When they are in tune, and working well their effect can be most beneficial.

Older civilisations were most conscious of these energies, and were most careful when placing their houses and religious sites. Our modern cultural attitudes tend to consider the planet as a plaything for mankind, and the energy lines in many places have become disrupted by our ignorant bumblings. It is within our power to husband these lines, and we should do so for in essence they are part of a universal network of energy, and all that means in terms of energy, intelligence, knowledge and light.

As regards the cottage site, all was not well there, but I don't feel that this is the time nor the place to list what was found, nor how the corrections were made. It is enough to say that when the work was completed we all became aware of a calmer and more peaceful atmosphere. The site was balanced and my task completed. It was time to leave and let the site achieve its designed purpose, whatever that might be.

HEALING: by Cyril Jarman.

A nurse by profession, Cyril's specialist training is in the nursing of the mentally ill and the terminally ill. Cured of arthritis by the healing process, he discovered his own healing talents and became a member of the National Federation of Spiritual Healing in 1982.

Since there has been man there has been spiritual healing. It is the true link between man and his creator and has been in existence for thousands of years, no one faith or religion can claim a monopoly.

The true healer is a person working irrespective of colour, class or creed and is a true spiritual person, in tune with the source of all creation. We all have our ways of interpreting the healing process. As I see it, the linking of the patient to his God or his soul, forms with the healer, a triangle of attunement that enables the healing energies from a divine source to flow.

There is only one source of energy and that is the Father-/Mother/God One-ness. We may experience it in different forms such as heat, electricity, gravity, healing, light, love and so on, even as disease. We cannot create or destroy it, but we can use the power of our thoughts to change the form in which it manifests in our lives.

Healers have different ways of perceiving their own talent. Some feel actual heat in their hands as they are working. Others use a visualisation process in which a mental picture of the affliction is symbolically treated. There are many different ways.

The National Federation of Spiritual Healers is a registered charity founded in 1955. It co-ordinates, protects and advances the work of spiritual healing. It is non-denominational, and accepts for membership all those who produce, over a period of time, evidence of a healing talent. 'Spiritual Healing' is understood to mean all forms of healing whether by 'touch' (ie. the laying on of hands), or prayer, or meditation. It may or may not be in the actual presence of the patient.

106

MEDIUMSHIP: by Evelyn Payne.

As a member of the Spiritualist National Union of Great Britain, Eve has practiced widely throughout this country, and abroad. She has run workshops and training courses in mediumship and spiritual philosophy for many years. She has been a natural medium since childhood, and is able to 'read' ley lines and ancient buildings.

A medium is a person who creates an invisible bridge between several layers of their inner and outer levels of consciousness before they commence their chosen field of work.

If we add to the basic material inborn psychic abilities, we now have a person who is capable of relaying messages from outside sources to an enquirer. In such a case the medium, to be able to work correctly, often has no previous knowledge of the subject matter.

A medium, as a general rule, has trained the psychic abilities up to the level of consciousness which then gives access into 'other worlds'. There they can make contact with deceased souls who could be members of a close family unit, or, souls similar to the Reverend William Thomas.

Mediums have been able to prove that a person's memory, character, and their feelings can, and do, survive physical death. If these souls have a caring nature on earth, that is, a sense of oneness, they do not shed that part of their nature when they make that final journey across the bridge between one life and the next. If they choose to bring back to earth a desire to help the people of earth within their own, individual skills, they are faced with a considerable problem. Being no longer resident in a physical body they can now only relay information to their chosen source via somebody else's physical body, ie. a medium. The main problem that they have to face is that they are operating on a faster frequency than does the average mind of earth. A medium, still living within the physical nature provides the necessary link or bridge, which has the power to balance various fields of energy into one working stream.

In parts of our invisible body can be found seven energy centres sited quite close to the major glandular organs. Each of these have valuable work to do in co-operating with their physical counterparts. When working, a mental medium operates, in the main, through the throat centre and the one which is found in the centre of the forehead. The throat produces the correct linking energy for the creation and outflow of clairaudience (the sense of hearing).

While the centre spot in the forehead provides the necessary energy to produce clairvoyance (the sense of seeing visions). A medium also uses the centre which is to be found aligned to our hearts. This produces the sense of feeling, as for example when a medium says 'I feel' something which has been sensed from an outside source. If a medium says that they 'feel' something that you are suffering from they are reading your Aura, your energy field. In other circumstances a medium could also be reading information from your own mind, either the 'surface' mind, or the deeper 'inner' mind. Mediums who work with cards, or palms, or with a crystal ball are often experts at mind reading.

The Aura, in simple terms, is a field of energy of three distinct levels which swirl around the body. It can be photographed using a special process. Clairvoyantly it is viewed as a whirling mixture of colours provided from a variety of sources. These colours and their shading tell a medium a great deal about your state of health, past illnesses and state of mind. The colour and intensity of the light that it sheds also give strong indications of a person's spiritual growth, or lack of growth. Within another layer could be found much of the past, and far past history of the subject (ie. reincarnation). To work to such a degree in this field requires additional training and an awful lot of time simply because, once again, we would be working through the sensory nature which is an area of our consciousness which does not recognise a physical time clock. So do not expect all the mediums that you meet to be skilled in this particular area.

My world is a fascinating one to live and work in and is filled with bright colours and a great deal of love and understanding. Many people enter its realms quite naturally through their instinctive or inspirational nature. They are the caring souls of this world. But please do not think that only mediums are psychic. It has been a common talent throughout the whole of the race of man since the beginning of time.

CONCLUSION : by the Author

The reader may be curious to know if, after all these psychic experiences, I believe in God.

As a child I believed in him as a literal and real person living in heaven, and I said my prayers to him, and was glad he was there. Today I see God in everything, both good and bad (or what we *call* bad), or beautiful and ugly (or what we *call* ugly). To me the word 'God' means a confusion of things, and I don't like to use the word any more because, for me, it has the limitations of my childhood. It's meaning is confined by what I was taught, and makes no allowance for the vastness I have since found out. Today I would prefer to use the term 'life force', which seems to be the most common and yet the most accurate one in use today.

I feel that I have, over the years of experience and exploration, learned to tap into that life force which is both inside and outside my physical body. I am only now beginning to see the great potential that this life force has once it is understood and used. From the inspirations I have received from William Thomas it is clear that this force is within everyone, within every living animal, within every plant and stone, within the very planet Earth itself. It was within the earliest of Earth's inhabitants, and they were aware of it's power and how to use it for the development of physical life upon the planet. Over the aeons we have lost touch with the life force, and glean only vague glimpses of how it was once used, from the few scattered remnants of aboriginal tribes that still exist. Our Earthly affairs are in a poor state today, but there is an awakening. I am a part of it and I now meet many, many other people who are also aware of it.

Wake up teachers! Wake up priests! Wake up people everywhere!

Post Script

by the Author

Through a connection I have recently made with a local healing centre, on 14th April, 1989, I received a piece of written information which was contained in a New Age Newsletter originating from America. It disclosed details of an imminent major energy introduction to all major power sites of the world.

A spiritual organization in Texas had been asked by the 'Ascended Masters' to lead this sacred world event. (I understand The Masters to be highly evolved souls working in areas of worldwide destiny). Besides Houston which is an important power centre, twelve other sacred places around the planet were to be activated on 16th April, 1989.

The Newsletter urged people of a spiritual awakening to gather upon known power sites around the world on the 16th of April to anchor the higher energies which were to be given to the earth.

Having read this article, Brian, John and I came to the conclusion that it had reached us, just in time, for a reason. We made the decision that we would return to the site of our old cottage on the morning of Sunday 16th April and as the article instructed, form a triangle of three people upon that ancient power site to anchor the energies.

To decide to return to the cottage required a degree of emotional courage from Brian and I. We had already been there once since leaving and had found it heartbreaking to look at in its state of deriliction. The Sunday morning was damp and misty and as we approached the cottage up the long driveway, the total devastation of that once beautiful garden and cottage broke my heart and I had to fight back the tears of anger that arose in me. It was now seven months since we had left. The cottage had been totally vandalized and looked sad and unloved. As I gazed upon it, memories of all that had taken place whilst we lived there came flooding back. I could hear the voices of the children and the barking of our playful dogs. I could remember the warm sunny days spent in those once so peaceful surroundings. In an attempt to balance my emotions I then fought to remember the hard times experienced there and then compared them to my feelings today in the peace of our beautiful farm environment. We had served our purpose on that site and had now moved on to a new stage in our lives. It is so easy when one looks back, just to remember the good times, but life is always a mix of good and bad. Thinking on these things, I could also find some good within the scene I was looking upon. Amid the dereliction there were still trees that we had left behind that were now in full blossom, and the bluebells were still growing out of the banks just as they had been upon the first day that we moved there sixteen years prior.

We walked around the interior of the cottage. The carpets we had left behind were sodden for there were gaping holes in the thatch and the slates had been removed from the rest of the roof. Vandals had stolen stone from the internal walls, bathroom and kitchen fittings had been smashed, and light fixtures ripped from the ceilings. Water was dripping from broken pipe work in every room and the floors were strewm with rubble.

We knew the centre of the hallway in the cottage to be the centre of the old stone circle. I felt instictively that we should hold hands together there and form a triangle to anchor the energies down into that ancient site on this important day for mankind. Onto the floor between the three of us I lay a bunch of bluebells which I had rescued from the garden. The three of us stood there in silence, lost deep within our own thoughts. I felt immense love for the piece of earth upon which I stood. I now recognised its importance and in my mind I welcomed the energies drawn down into it. We had rebalanced that site ready for just such an event as was taking place today. It was now ready for the coming of the New Age and for the energies which were being received through the major earth power sites that would have an influence upon every power site across the world.

As I stood engrossed within my thoughts, I sensed a build up of people around us within the etheric. I could feel as many as thirty people crowding around us and I knew instictively that they had loving connections to the site and the old cottage.

As we stepped outside to leave I realised that sadness had left me. It seemed uncanny that building development had not commenced yet, making it possible for us to return, undisturbed, to that ancient site to anchor the energies. For that day the site was mine, although I no longer owned it in the worldly sense.